The ceiling bulged upward and the floor began to tilt

There was a roar in his ears. His chair started to roll. He clung to it for support, but it hurled him off.

Throughout the chaos he could hear his own voice screaming, "They doped me! They fixed my drink!"

He tried to get up, but he was shaking too hard and the floor kept moving away.

Then his lungs stopped working and his voice stopped screaming. And the whole room shimmered as he rocketed off into infinity.

THE WHEEL IS FIXED

James M. Fox

A RAVEN HOUSE MYSTERY FROM

W🌐RLDWIDE

TORONTO • LONDON • NEW YORK • SYDNEY

Raven House edition published February 1982

Second printing February 1982

ISBN 0-373-63022-0

1

HERE AT THE CORTEZ HOTEL in El Paso I am registered as Donald Wells, but my real name is Richard Bailey, and I am a fugitive from justice.

That is what they are calling us on page two of the first section of this morning's *Herald-Express*. It took me a little while to find it, after I'd peeled off the Sunday comics and shaken out the weekly rotos and the local society junk and thirty-six pages of classified ads. It is only a quarter column with a brief, inaccurate rehash of the messy part, and the headline says tersely: Hunt Couple in Palm Springs Swim Pool Massacre. It mentions that the F.B.I. is after us; they found the car in Phoenix yesterday, which proves we crossed a state line and makes us eligible for five years in the federal penitentiary right there. It describes Lorna as a motion picture actress, which she is not, and me as a salesman, which probably means they've found out about those three weeks last year when I toted a suitcase load of greeting cards around the streets of Hollywood.

The Aston Martin may have saved our skins, last Friday night. It was very fast, nothing but a long gray hood packed solid with power. They

didn't know we had it, and once we got under
way we were across the Arizona line at Blythe
before they could get the alarm out, maybe even
before they missed us. There were three hundred
miles of open desert, and the harsh white beam
of our headlights stabbing the dark, and the rank
smell of leather and hot motor oil, and the high-
pitched whine of our tires, the growl of the exhaust, the nerve-wracking scream of a leaky
muffler. It was something like trying to escape
from a nightmare on the crest of a tornado.

We covered those three hundred miles in less
than four hours and made it to Phoenix just
before midnight.

She never said a word. She huddled away from
me on her side of the seat, nursing her bandaged
hands in her lap. The green reflection of the
dashboard lights gave me an occasional glimpse
of her face in the strange pale composure of ex-
treme shock, eyes closed, lips tightly pressed and
sometimes twitching gently, cheeks like pools of
deep blue shadow. She made the perfect picture
of a beautiful young murderess riding off into
purgatory, and I loved her more intensely than a
man with a rope around his neck loves life itself.

I don't know how they missed us coming into
the city. Perhaps they were looking for us on the
Interstate, whereas I had taken the detour
around Wickenburg through Sun City and arrived on Route 89. More likely they never expected us to get this far in the first place, or, if
we did, to dare drive straight into town. It was an
idiotic risk to take, but it would have been just as
dangerous to abandon the car on the highway

and hitchhike in together. So we took it and came sliding down Main Street with our broken muffler sputtering away like a submachine gun and nobody paying the slightest attention to us.

I pulled up a block beyond the Greyhound Bus depot and backed into an alley and sneaked into the station from the rear to check on schedules. There was an eastbound bus leaving at 1:20 A.M. I bought a ticket to Kansas City, and the man told me I'd have to change at El Paso. Then I went back to the car and gave Lorna the ticket and told her to wait in the ladies' room until a few minutes before bus time. I hadn't noticed any cops in the station, but it was important, of course, that we should not be seen together if we were going to have any kind of chance at all.

It was terribly awkward, as well, with her hands in such bad shape she could hardly use them, bandaged fingertips more hopelessly conspicuous than the mark of Cain. Her own gloves would have killed her, if she'd brought any, but I had a pair of elderly yellow pigskins in my overcoat pocket that would just barely fit without pressure. They looked clumsy on her, and a little ridiculous in combination with the plain green raw silk suit she was wearing. The suit was a Dior item that would have retailed at four figures. I didn't think she'd be likely to run into anybody who might know about that. I fished a twenty-dollar lipstick from her green morocco shoulder-strap purse and used it on her, rather shakily, and helped her out of the car, and watched her walk stiffly down the block to the depot, push the door open with her elbow and disappear inside. If nobody happened to see the look in her eyes she'd pass for just another fairly attractive young woman on a quick emergency trip back home because of death in the family.

The Aston Martin's fuel gauge said empty. It had been saying that for the past twenty miles, but when I touched the starter there was still a whine of response left in the supercharger, enough to drag me three blocks across town and down the asphalt ramp into the basement garage of the Westward Ho. The night attendant, a brisk young Mexican in spotless white overalls, didn't seem to be curious or particularly impressed. I told him I was catching a plane for L.A. and I'd be back on Monday to pick up the car. I didn't expect to fool them, but it might gain us half an hour while they checked the airport.

Then I ducked into an all-night coffeepot around the corner and choked down a ham sandwich and a cup of coffee. There were a couple of cab drivers at the other end of the counter, and a well-dressed drunk knocking himself out on the illegal nickel grabber, swearing under his breath at every lemon. He was a tall, long-nosed party in neatly pressed brown gabardine, with a real Panama on the back of his neck and a sweaty flush of exertion on his shallow jowls from slaving away on the handle bar. I could tell by the buzz-*click* of the wheels that the house had rollered off practically all but a couple of cherries, and the guy figured about as likely to win as I figured walking out of this jam on my feet, but we both kept on trying anyway. I got the porter who was sweeping out the joint aside, and passed him a fifty, and had him run over to the bus depot for a ticket to Amarillo, Texas. He didn't ask questions, he just put his broom away and shuffled off. Before I'd finished my sandwich he was back with the ticket and a handful of change. I tipped him, paid the check, scowled at the drunk getting on my nerves, and made for the depot as fast as I could without actually running.

The waiting room was dimly lighted; the big clock above the exit to the stage platform said 12:43. Two sailors were sleeping on a bench, and a very young couple in faded jeans and starched calico were fussing over a baby in a brand-new pink plastic traveling cradle. I had some trouble keeping my eyes off the ladies' door, and picked a seat that let me turn my back on it as long as I leaned an arm on Lorna's bag, the first I'd snatched from her closet and chucked a few of her things into on our way out. I knew we should have at least one piece of luggage, but this one wasn't much use. It was too small and too expensive, an oversize weekend case in polished alligator with gold-plated locks. Still, it would have to do, and at least it served better for carrying the money than Hitchcock's flimsy and rather obvious black satchel.

The minutes stumbled by like tired old men lugging boxes of dynamite. Around one o'clock a few more people drifted into the waiting room from the street. Most of them were just the usual local night-owl types, come to kibitz the show. A grizzled old jockey in a greasy white coat opened up the lunch counter and laid out a small stack of magazines and a batch of early-morning *News*

Chronicles. I strolled over to buy one; the headline was something about the energy crisis, but
they had a smudged-up bulletin under stop press
on the front page: "Four Slain in Palm Springs
Gang Battle." The bulletin made no reference to
us at all, or to the money, either.

At 1:06 the big gray diesel stage pulled into the
station with a snort and a squeal of air brakes,
and proceeded to spill a trickle of passengers. My
hands squeezed into fists when the khaki uniform came swaggering in, but it was only the
driver walking through to the locker room, looking for his relief man. Then I really went tense all
over, because right on his heels were two burly
customers in slacks and horse-blanket sports
coats, reasonable facsimiles of Sergeant Dettlinger and his partner. I swung away from them,
dropping my newspaper and almost toppling Lorna's suitcase off the bench, and they passed me
less than three feet away, strolling on out
through the exit into the street. They were talking crops, and their voices had a tired Arizona
drawl, nothing like Dettlinger's hard city accent.

The dispatcher's loudspeaker started crackling
and announced that number twenty-one from
Los Angeles was now loading for El Paso, Fort
Worth, Dallas, Little Rock and Memphis, all
aboard, please. People drifted back to the platform; the two sailors and the couple with the
baby were already on the bus. I caught myself
watching the ladies' door and grinding my teeth.
At last it opened, slowly, and she slipped out
across the room, looking very pale but carrying
herself easily, almost proudly. A tall, rangy

fellow in a Stetson and fancy Western boots held
the door to the platform for her. He spoke to her
and she remembered to smile at him.

I got up and followed her at a safe distance.
She'd found a seat by herself, halfway down,
when I boarded the stage. The relief driver
glanced at my ticket from behind the wheel and
waved me on impatiently. He did not even notice
the bag. I picked a seat up front and shoved the
bag out of sight under it, and let go of my breath
when the air brakes hissed. We were rolling east
again.

It's hard to imagine how I could have dozed off
for almost an hour under those conditions, but
the next thing I knew, my wristwatch showed
2:14 and something had happened to jar me back
into spine-prickling apprehension. I couldn't
figure it out right away, because the bus was still
droning along through the night at a normal fifty-
five, and most of the passengers were sprawling
asleep in their seats with only two pinpoint lights
burning dimly overhead. Then my ears caught a
snatch of Lorna's whisper, harsh with subdued
distress, and I saw she wasn't alone anymore: the
tall Westerner now sat beside her, one long arm
possessively lodged around her shoulders. His
grin did not leave me the slightest doubt about
the purpose of the conversation. I set my teeth
and called myself seventeen different kinds of
idiot, and then I remembered she could not even
use her hands. I stumbled down the stage's swaying aisle and stood up facing them, keeping the
snarl out of my voice with an effort. "This man
annoying you, miss?"

She looked up at me with dark, frightened eyes that implored me to be careful. "No, thank you. I'm... it's all right. Don't bother." The whisper was so low I had to read her trembling lips.

He was staring at me with marked derision, openly curious. "What's riding you, partner? Got yore brand on the little lady?" He did not move his arm, nor hide the insult in his lazy drawl.

I told him no brand, and I couldn't even ask him to step outside, but the driver could, if that was the way he wanted it. The baby in the plastic traveling cradle woke up and promptly started bawling. The two sailors in the next seat woke up in turn, took in the situation at a glance and offered impartially sarcastic comment. Other voices joined in a surly chorus of protest; the driver took his foot off the gas and glared at us in his mirror. The lanky Westerner got up slowly, gave me a nasty smirk and retired to his own seat. I went back to mine, not trusting myself to look at Lorna anymore. I was cold all over and shaking with nerves. I'd had a glimpse of what our life was going to be like, even if we did get away with it.

The Stetson gallant got off the stage at Lordsburg, where we stopped for breakfast at 6:00 A.M. Most of the passengers stayed aboard, squinting at the hard, brassy ball of the sun rising above the rocky tableland. There was a crackle of waxed paper and a smell of food parcels and thermoses behind me, and the baby set up another howl. I pretended to doze through it all and listened to Lorna's cool, weary voice politely refusing to share the sailors' supply of victuals.

The driver came back, zipping up his pants. He hoisted himself behind the wheel again and leaned on his horn in a blast of warning to stragglers. Two very old Indians huddling in a doorway and a lone horseman on a buckskin pony watched us pull out into the highway.

It was close to noon on Saturday when we came rumbling through the streets of El Paso and swung into the busy junction depot. The northbound stage for Amarillo, Tulsa, Kansas City and Chicago was already drawn up on the adjoining platform. I strolled into the waiting room, carrying the fancy little alligator bag. There were no uniforms around, no loiterers hiding behind a newspaper. Lorna came in, pale and drawn from exhaustion, still wearing my old yellow gloves. By daylight they gave her just the right touch of dowdiness.

I pushed the revolving door to the street for her and followed her out. There was no taxi stand, but I snagged a passing cab and put her in it with the bag. It was another deadly risk to take, but she didn't look fit to walk a block, and it was the only way in which she could take luggage into the hotel without actually carrying it herself. I had already told her what to do when she got there.

The cab went off with her, and I followed on foot. The Cortez has a drugstore; I remembered the place from playing the Crystal Room, just about the last stretch I'd done with my own band before painting myself into a corner. There was a crowd for the early-luncheon rush hour, but I managed to get my hands on a glass of milk, a chocolate bar and a couple of doughnuts: anything for some quick energy. When she'd had

twenty minutes or so to get settled and dismiss
the bellhop, I ducked into a phone booth, called
the hotel operator and asked for Mrs. Mary Hendricks.

The delay and the whispered consultation at
the private branch exchange curled my hair.
Something clicked on the line and a male voice
broke in, mentioned a number. I tried breathing
and discovered it helped. The operator said she
was sorry to keep me waiting, my party had only
just checked in.

"Rick?"

"Yes. Are you all right?"

"I think so. It's 1264. I feel sort of weak."

"Call room service. You've got to eat something. I'll be right up."

The registration clerk wore neatly tailored
frontier pants and a hand-embroidered rancher's
shirt in yellow and black, but he looked just as
bored as any other hotelman. He didn't look as if
he'd have noticed that she could hardly hold a
pen, or that there was anything odd about those
gloves. He said it was a dull weekend, lucky for
me, dropping in without reservation. Yes, he had
some space higher up, a single on ten and a suite
on twelve. He didn't seem particularly surprised
that a guest who needed a shave and his clothes
pressed would want the suite. I told him my luggage was at the airport, all I'd come in for was a
few hours' sleep and to see a couple of people in
town. He merely nodded, took my money and
snapped a finger at the bell captain.

I drew 1259 and spent five minutes washing up
and scraping the fur off my face with the razor

and some brushless cream I'd bought at the drugstore. Then I crossed the corridor, scratched on
1264 and walked in. She was lying on the bed, as
limp as a broken doll.

"You've ordered lunch?"

"Not yet. My hands...."

I took off the gloves very carefully and removed the bandages. Most of her fingers were in
terrible shape, but it was the kind of thing where
calling a doctor meant you might just as well
phone the cops yourself. I broke out the rest of
my drugstore supplies: ointment and fresh gauze
and a bottle of aspirin.

"Rick, I'm so sorry...."

"It's okay."

"I had no right to drag you into it."

"Listen, I was in it from the start. The whole
thing was my fault. You can stop worrying about
that part of it. What you need is food, and a few
hours' sleep. We'll cross the border tonight and
get married in Mexico. From there on in it'll be
fairly plain sailing."

"I think we should go back."

"You *what*?"

She winced and squeezed her eyelids tightly
closed. They were like hollow bruises smashed
into her by a savage fist. I bit my lips, hard
enough to taste blood, and slipped the gloves
back over the new bandages.

"We can make it," I said cheerfully. "It's just a
question of money now, and money's the least of
our troubles. Mexico City tomorrow, a change of
clothes, a change of papers—everything we
need, at a price. Then South America, Italy, the

French Riviera, anyplace we like. They tell you
it's a small world, they don't know what they're
talking about. Four thousand million people. I'm
growing a mustache, and you can be a redhead
and wear sloppy clothes. I'll bet you've always
wanted that."

"Have I?" She forced a smile. "South America. ... Rick, do you love me still? In spite of—
everything?"

"Could you possibly doubt it?"

"Yes. Tell me again. I need to hear you tell me."

"I love you. Very much. Now listen, you've
absolutely got to snap out of this and take care of
yourself. I'll run you a hot bath, and you call
room service and have them send up something
light and nourishing, like a chicken liver omelet.
And a quart of milk, with a pony of rum for a
chaser. I'll help you undress, and I'll feed you, if
necessary—you mustn't use those hands except
in an emergency. Then you're off to bed while I
go out to make a few inquiries."

"All right." She did not look at me.

There wasn't any real point in making inquiries. I knew the local setup, and I'd visited
Mexico before. You're supposed to get a tourist
card from the consulate and pass customs inspection, but here in El Paso nobody bothers. Local
traffic goes back and forth across four bridges
over the Rio Grande into Juarez on the other
side, and the Mexicans consider it all just one big,
happy family, unless you're going to try to drive
up with a truckload of contraband. This creates a
pretty nice arrangement, in some cases. All I
needed was to check the deal.

Downstairs the air-conditioned lobby was cool, dark and quiet with the comfortable seclusion of all good hotel parlors. Outside the plaza lay baking and shimmering in the muggy afternoon heat and offered the harsh anonymity of the weekend crowds. At the first intersection a khaki-shirted cop grabbed my shoulder when I tried to make a dash for the Juarez streetcar. I hadn't even noticed him, and my knees lurched under me; for one awful second I staggered against him before I managed to brace myself. He was tall as I am, a husky young six-footer, his brick-red tan creased tight into a formidable scowl. He wore a shiny new silver badge with a high number, but the .45 on his carefully polished cartridge belt sagged professionally down the hips.

"Where you from, stranger?"

I told him New York City, barely subduing the croak that wanted to ride my tongue, and he loosened his grip.

"We got crosswalks for pedestrians heah, for yore own protection. We don't want y'all to get hurt in this heah city. Whatcha nervous about anyways?"

"Sorry, officer. You startled me. I didn't know."

He shrugged and released my shoulder and pointed to the crosswalk ten yards away. The trolley was still there, waiting for the lights. I climbed aboard on brittle wooden legs and dropped half my change on the floor paying the fare. The Mexican motorman showed me a toothy grin. "*Dedos de hilacha, señor?*"

Butterfingers? Yes, indeed. I ignored him and

pushed toward the rear of the car. It carried a
near-capacity load, mostly of overalled workmen
and elderly women shoppers in cotton serapes,
but there was a sprinkling of tourists—two
paunchy, middle-aged types with cameras, a
freckled young man reading a copy of *This Week
in El Paso*, and a pretty dark brunette with a
white linen dress who toted one of those flat
wooden cases artists use for carrying their
sketching supplies.

When the trolley groaned around the curve
onto the bridge approach I dropped off and
watched it rumble onto the bridge. On the sidewalk two Indian women had spread their wares,
and I had to pretend some interest in blankets
and pottery as a cover for hanging around. The
trolley hit the bridge, slowed down and squealed
to an unscheduled stop in front of the little
customs shack on the American side, where they
normally halt only incoming traffic. Two men in
Panama hats and sleekly tailored brown gabar-
dines boarded the car. They walked through it
and jumped off again, bringing the freckled lad
and the young artist out with them. The trolley
waited while the sketching case was being
opened and the girl's purse inspected; the man
produced his wallet and showed papers. Everybody seemed to be quite casual about it all, and I
was close enough to catch a shred of the girl's
laughter as she got back on the trolley, assisted
by her fellow victim. The motorman clanged his
bell complacently and the men in the Panama
hats waved him on his way. At the shack the
uniformed customs officer on duty shifted his

back off the wall and spat reflectively to leeward over the bridge balustrade. Fifty yards up the bridge, with its rear wheels touching the boundary line, a plain black sedan with a long buggy-whip antenna hugged the curbside. It was too far away for me to see who might be in it, mostly because I was already crossing the street and walking back into the city just as fast as could be managed with decorum.

Lorna was in bed, still wide awake, staring at the ceiling. I dropped into a chair by the open window and looked at the view—the clean white battlement of rooftops and terraces, the glittering corkscrew thread of the river, the parched brown foothills reaching far beyond.

"You've got to get some sleep."

"Yes. I know."

"I'll find you a couple of pills. We can't leave tonight. Not until you're in better shape."

"I'll be all right."

"No, it's like this. Mexico is out. They're watching the bridges."

"Oh. . . ."

"It doesn't mean anything. I don't think they know we're here yet. Closing the border is an easy routine in a case like this. They'll check the airlines and the railroad, of course."

"I see."

"Don't worry. We can still make it. They can't block all the roads. Not until they've actually narrowed down the search to this area, and even then it's a hell of a job. I'm going out again the minute you're asleep to buy a good used car, borrow a couple of dealer's license plates for a day or two. Tomorrow night we're pulling out of here with the weekend crowd. We'll be in New Orleans by Tuesday morning, a cool thousand miles across country. I've got friends there who know the ropes, who can put us up and get us on a Caribbean freighter for a few hundred bucks, without any nonsense. That's all there is to it.''

"All right."

I turned around and frowned at her, and she barely smiled back at me. Against the white pillow there was little more of her than a stain of black curls and darkly shadowed eyes. I went over and felt her brow, pressed the veins of her arms. "Does that hurt?"

"No."

"Be right back with the snooze dope."

She took two, meekly as a small child. "Rick, don't go. . . ."

"What's wrong?"

"Nothing. Hold me, darling. I'll go to sleep if you stay with me."

"I was going to."

She was too tired and too self-conscious about her hands to reach for me. "Please, Rick. I'm frightened by myself. Don't leave me anymore."

"Take it easy. I'm not even supposed to be here at all. A little thing like the maid coming in with towels could settle our hash. You won't know I'm gone, honey."

"Yes, I will. I *will* know it. Rick, tell me again!"

"I love you. I love you so much it hurts. I don't give a damn if you killed the guy. I don't care if you *were* Vanni's mistress, or Fidel Castro's. You belong to me now and it's going to stay that way."

The haunted dark blue eyes flickered at me and changed to violet and closed gently. When she was breathing regularly in my arms I laid her back on the pillow and quietly drew the curtains. I left the room on tiptoes and hung out the Do Not Disturb sign, and went out again.

Buying a car was almost too simple. At the lot on Alameda I had to make myself pretend that I wasn't a suspiciously easy mark. I even forced myself to do a little haggling. The salesman took one look at my roll and eagerly agreed to lend me a pair of plates for the weekend. He sold me a conservative gray Chrysler Cordoba that was only a few months old. He filled it up for me himself and drove it on the grease rack and supervised the mechanic who gave it a lube job. He made out a bill of sale to Donald Wells, of Des Moines, Iowa, took my money and almost jumped to attention when I drove off.

I parked in an all-night garage two blocks from the Cortez, had a snack in the coffee shop and looked in on Lorna before returning to my own quarters. She was sleeping peacefully, even snoring a little, completely relaxed. The hideous yellow gloves were below the sheet. She did not look like a murderess anymore; she was a small, uncommonly beautiful child who had been very sick, but who was going to be allowed to sit up tomorrow and play with her dolls. I wanted to smile at her, but I couldn't quite make it, being a hundred years old myself and barely able to walk without crutches.

But something tells me that this is no show. Any gambler develops an instinct that warns him when he hasn't got a prayer. I've chucked away hands with four kings in them and dropped the dice as if they'd scorched me after six straight passes. Only this time the house won't let me quit, and I don't mean Sergeant Dettlinger, or the F.B.I., or the California courts, either. A murder rap is something you can beat, or any good attorney can, and we'd always be able to make out a pretty fair case of self-defense if a jury should ever get to hear it. If we should live that long.

So I am spending today in writing down how it happened, all of it. Maybe I can hide the result somewhere, such as under the seat of the car, where the cops will find it, but where *they* won't bother to look. The newspapers and TV and true-crime magazines will have a field day with it; the lawyers and the politicians will call it a confession. But at least the truth will be known, and the deal will have to be from the top of the deck.

2

I⊤ STARTED LAST MONDAY. I had a room in an old
clapboard flytrap motel in East Hollywood that
called itself the Sierra Lagos, where they gave
me a special weekly rate and didn't always lock
me out if I got a day or two behind. I owned a suit
of clothes, a pair of shoes, two shirts, two sets of
underwear in bad repair and eighty-two cents
cash. The car I drove around was a '66 Ford. I
couldn't have sold that, or hocked it, either; not
for more than fifty dollars. Anyway, in California even a bum has to have wheels.

When the manager knocked on my door around
noon and shouted something about a man on the
phone, I thought at first it was a gag, because not
even Marion was supposed to know where I
lived. It was that kind of an address, and there
were other reasons. Then I got up after all and
put some clothes on and went down to see for
myself. The phone was a rusty coin-box affair on
the wall under the stairs. It talked to me impatiently in a clipped, high-class European accent.
It said that this was Mr. Kovacs, who was speaking for Mr. Walter Hitchcock, and invited me to
see Mr. Hitchcock that same afternoon at three
o'clock on a matter of business.

I got quite a bang out of that. I knew I'd been a bad boy who was due for a spanking, but it hardly seemed like a case for the Board of Education. I said so after I got my breath back, and Mr. Kovacs sneered at me in agreement. He informed me that this was about a job.

There wasn't much else I could say except "Oh," and promise to be on deck at three. He told me where and hung up. I put a dime in the slot to call Marion at her office, which left me seventy-two cents for drugstore orange juice and sinkers, standard Hollywood bum fare. She sounded snippier than usual, after last night's fight about one thing and another.

"Isn't this pretty early for you to be up and around?"

"Yes. I guess it is."

"Rick, I can't talk now. People are waiting to see me, and there goes my other phone. You can call me later this afternoon."

"Just a second. I may not be here this afternoon."

"What do you mean?"

"Man called me up just now and offered me a job."

Her tone changed instantly. "Isn't that wonderful! Darling, I'm so happy for you. . . . But it's here in town, isn't it? Which man, Rick?"

"The name's Hitchcock. You don't know him."

"Walter Hitchcock, who owns all those hotels?"

"That's right."

"Of course I know him, silly. We used to handle some of his publicity. Oh, Rick, that's grand! What sort of a job?"

"He didn't say. Look, I may have to go away

for a while. Don't worry if you don't hear from me the next couple of weeks, and don't talk about it, will you, sweetheart?"

"Why can't I? Rick, you're making this up!" she accused me heatedly.

It was reasonable enough for her to think so, and very unreasonable of me to slam the phone on the hook. I wasn't mad at her or anything, I just didn't want to have another fight. I went back upstairs and finished dressing and sat around trying to figure things out on an empty stomach.

I forget who told me the story, but the way I heard it they had a serious meat shortage in Germany back in 1921, and in the town of Hanover a butcher named Haarmann was arrested for selling steaks and chops off carefully selected two-legged carcasses. When the news hit New York there were quite a few citizens who hustled into court to see about swapping the family name for something that would sound a little less indelicate, and among them was a small-time Park Avenue bootlegger, Josef Haarmann. The German handle cramped his style anyway, with his particular type of clientele, and the change improved business prospects to a point where he was able to hold his own with outfits like those of Dutch Schultz and Legs Diamond, who were less interested in the private carriage trade than in the massive nightclub and speakeasy markets. By the time repeal came around things were different; the depression had already creamed off most of his profits, and the only place where people still carried wallets and checkbooks was out West.

He arrived in California in the spring of '34, opened a string of liquor stores and went bank-

rupt within six months, the lucrative kind of
bankruptcy. With his profits he bought a piece of
the old Reno syndicate and started working his
way through college. Before Pearl Harbor he and
his son, Walter, had it all neatly wrapped up: the
cops, the lawyers and the politicians, the bookies
and the wire services, the plush casinos and the
little dark-town social clubs, the coin-machine
routes and the punchboard routes and the tipster
sheets, the whole elaborate network of lottery-
ticket salesmen and numbers-game pools, everything snug and cozy and strictly on the square,
with all the flimflam boys and the hophead trig-
gers crowded outside looking in.

By 1953 they were in the hotel business from
Cuba clear across to Honolulu. They had to find
some way of laundering the stuff and beating out
the I.R.S. on capital depreciation. The old man
turned in his chips about that time, and Walter
had become the senior regional executive of the
whole operation. He and his associates were
rumored not to care for deadbeats very much
themselves. It was supposed to make them cross
when anyone would try to pull something—such
as, for instance, sign a piece of paper that would
come back from the bank in a few days, neatly
endorsed in purple, "No Account."

Getting out of town wasn't going to be easy,
not on seventy-two cents. I could thumb a ride
east, but that was a slow business, and it was
exactly what they'd expect me to do. Maybe they
would be satisfied to let me go, but if they were
laying for me to make an example I wouldn't get
very far that way. They had organized them-

selves a thousand miles of territory west of the
Rockies, and they'd be likely to consider this a
question of prestige. They had Tijuana and
Acapulco sewed up, too. Then there was always
the Pacific Ocean. I picked up the Sunday paper
and checked out the shipping list. A Japanese
cargo liner was sailing at eight from Wilmington,
and a small Norwegian tub at midnight from San
Pedro. If I could shake them off that long. Then
again it was an odds-on bet that might be worse—
play stowaway or take a pistol whipping and be
done with it. I wasn't really far enough out of
line to rate much more than a couple of days in
the accident ward at County Hospital.

What bothered me was they would go all the
way up through channels to command level
about such a minor tactical operation as a rubber
check. They weren't kidding me about it, either.
They were generally discouraged from taking the
name of the Big Fellow in vain.

It didn't take a lot of nerve to make me decide
against running, after all. I'd picked up a Bronze
Star and a couple of Purple Hearts in the Army,
but even a cornered and hungry rabbit would
just as soon jump into the cooking pot by himself,
and in my case I knew full well that the only
party responsible for this awkward situation was
one Richard Bailey, 35, of White Plains, New
York, a musician of sorts by trade, but in more recent years a lousy, no-good, self-pitying petty
grifter with his very own self-starting private
jinx.

3

THE ADDRESS I'D BEEN GIVEN was in one of those quiet backwater canyons out in Bel Air, at least a mile north of Sunset Boulevard, where the building restrictions specify brick garden walls and no lots under five acres. I found an open gate featuring a set of flying cupids in heavy wrought iron and the initials W.H. inside a bronze laurel wreath. The black composition driveway curved away among the jacaranda trees. I was still wondering about whether to use it or park outside in the street when trumpet horns blared imperiously and a long, low-slung gray sports car swept around the curve with a roar and a whine of gears. It skidded out through the gate, casually clipped off one of my rusty fenders and screamed to a stop twenty yards behind me, nuzzling a lamp post.

I sat very still, watching the driver in my mirror. He had climbed out and came stalking me on stiff long legs like a terrier pup who's found an alley cat trespassing in his backyard. He was a tall, slender youth in designer jeans and a rather loud silk scarf, the blond, quasi-athletic type without any real coordination or hard muscle. The frustrated, emotional type that is considered handsome by all the girls and dated by few. His pale blue eyes were snapping at me and at the battered old Ford; his drawl had a tight, expensive, private-school quality tightly kept under control. "Manage to kill a lot of people with that junk pile of yours?"

He wasn't fooling. He really believed I had hit him, probably on purpose, and he resented it with an intensity that verged on tears of fury. I just sat there looking up at him. It stumped me how I was going to handle him. I mumbled something about insurance and he curled his lip for me.

"Don't tell me you can get insurance on that bucket."

"Take it easy, fellow," I said. "Maybe I'm not the one who needs it."

That was enough to set him off. He went white all over under his smooth coat of tan and called me a name that almost cracked his voice. He reached inside and grabbed a handful of my shirt and tried to haul me out through the window. He was so young and arrogant, so desperately unsure of himself, I didn't even have the heart to punch him in the nose.

"Something wrong, Mr. Stuart?"

There were two of them standing behind him. They had heard the crash, of course, and they were still breathing fast from running, but now they did not seem to be worried anymore. The one who looked like an Irish pug in chauffeur's blue serge cap and leggings had a familiar face—I couldn't place him accurately, but we had certainly been frequenting the same dice joints and horse parlors. The other one wore beautifully tailored summer tweeds and the deeply lined, faintly sinister features and glossy patent-leather hair, streaked with gray, of an elderly gigolo.

The blond youth let go of my shirt and scowled at them, his tantrum spent as quickly as it had come on. He shrugged and swaggered back to his car and drove off in a snarl of ruthlessly applied compressor thrust. The Irish chauffeur looked me over without much interest and nodded.

"Yeah, that's him," he said hoarsely, opening the door on my side. It snagged his coat and showed me the bulging holster on his belt.

The patent-leather kid jerked his head. I didn't know him, but I knew his accent, and the sneer that came with it.

"Thees way, Bailey. We haff been waiting for you already."

Mr. Walter Hitchcock reclined in the nude on a white sponge-rubber mattress by the side of his kidney-shaped, pink-tiled swimming pool. He had the flat, muscular body and the swarthy tan of a young Roman centurion, weirdly in contrast to the almost distinguished head of a retired British field marshal, complete with iron-gray military mustache, eagle nose and flashing, contemptuous, rust brown eyes. I didn't mind the raking those eyes gave me. I was almost dizzy with relief, listening to Kovacs's formal introduction. They were going to play this one for courtesy of the table, after all. They had an angle and they were dealing me in. In Hollywood the swimming pool is supposed to be a conference room; they keep their blackjacks out in the front office.

A Japanese houseboy came pussyfooting from the house with a trayload of Scotch and a silver ice jug. He brought me a gaily striped canvas director's chair and a trick ash stand shaped like a gnome. He offered cigars from a humidor with a music-box attachment that played the "Blue Danube" waltz for me. I took one just to be polite and for something to occupy my fingers; I needed a roast-beef sandwich, not a cigar. In the pool a large yellow rubber duck drifted lazily with the breeze, watching me from one sardonic red eye. The houseboy did a fadeout and Kovacs lounged against the diving board behind me, sneering into his highball.

"A piahno player," he said, tasting the words as if they were smeared with Limburgér.

Hitchcock ignored him. The harsh brown eyes raked me over some more.

"I hear you don't like California," he said. The tone was captain-of-industry, straight from the gravel pit. The skin between my shoulders started prickling again.

"California's all right," I said. "It's just my luck that needs a change of seasons."

"Talk sense, Bailey. Your luck can't sign its name on rubber. Don't you know what happens to welshers?"

There was nothing I could answer to that without sounding like an ass, so I let it go by. He knitted the coarse gray bristles that ran in one shaggy crest from temple to temple and inspected the evenly drawing cone of his cigar. "You're a professional musician?"

"Yeah, but I had a little trouble with the union."

Kovacs coughed eloquently. "Trobble," he said. "Maybe you don't know trobble when she's sitting in your lap."

I looked at him carefully over my shoulder. It wasn't a question of his words so much as of his manner. "Two thousand dollars," I said. "Okay, so it's a matter of policy with you gentlemen, and I'm a welsher. But that cashier at Louie's is a drunken bully, and if I hadn't given him a check there would've been a riot in the joint. It didn't seem worth it at the time. Sorry, but I don't see much point in your making all these cracks about *piahno* players, buddy."

He stared at me with that funny, venomous kind of hostility many of them still have in their blood from generations of feuding over some rocky patch of hillside land with a plum tree on it and a couple of goats grazing. Hitchcock brushed a fly off his stomach and snorted impatiently.

"I'll handle this, Steve," he said; and to me, "You want back in?"

"If you mean the music business," I said slowly, "the answer is obvious. But it would take a little something I don't happen to have lying around—such as, for instance, quite a piece of money. You see, my last engagement I managed to drop about two weeks' payroll for the boys. That was four years ago, and I've paid back some of it, but I'd have to find every cent before the union would consider playing ball with me again.''

"How much?''

I shrugged and told him. It was the kind of figure you remember much better than your own birthday. There wasn't any secret about it, either, but I couldn't see why they should be interested. He just nodded at me and said calmly, "It's a loan. You can open at the Royal-Columbus in Bermuda on the twenty-first of next month.''

"Huh?''

"Union scale plus twenty and expenses. For the season. Suit you?''

I swallowed my drink, fast, and rocked with the seesaw movement of the terrace under my chair. Dizziness wasn't the word for it.

"Listen, Mr. Hitchcock, it takes time to put a band in shape. I used to have connections—''

"You want the job?''

"Yeah, I want it,'' I said thickly, feeling Kovacs's sneer on the back of my neck and not daring to look at either of them.

"In Bermuda iss no games,'' said Kovacs, keeping me posted. "No bookies, yet. *Basta*. You weel not like that, moch.''

The cigar broke in my hand. I wanted to hit him, but the best I could do was a sickly grin. "Bermuda sounds just fine,'' I said. "This is all very handsome, and I do appreciate it. But maybe you gentlemen have something in mind about a way for me to return the favor?''

"You're supposed to get this bim out of my hair,'' said Hitchcock bluntly, without so much as blinking an eyelid.

The terrace stopped seesawing and the sun's reflection in the pool jumped back into focus. "Yes, sir," I said cheerfully. "Excuse me, please. I didn't catch that. Sounded like you wanted me to get a woman out of your hair."

"That's right."

We had ourselves a pause for station identification. I don't smoke hash or anything, and I knew where I was and who they were all the time. I didn't think they were just having fun. On the other hand, nothing short of Calamity Jane in person would be particularly likely to bother them at all. A good stiff overdose of sleeping pills would set them back about a dollar eight at the nearest cut-rate drugstore.

"Show him, Steve," said Hitchcock, glaring at me and my foolish suspicions.

Kovacs produced a little sheaf of folded documents. "These private matter, Bailey," he admonished me. "Very confidential. You smart man—too smart to talk, huh?" He smiled, as blandly as the grooves of dissipation in his rakish features would allow him.

It was a report from a private detective agency, the kind with sixty-seven offices in the western hemisphere and correspondents in all major cities of the world; the kind that serves bankers' associations, railroad companies, and royalty in exile. I couldn't make head or tail of it. It was neatly typed and impersonally worded, addressed to nobody in particular, and referred at length to someone, apparently female, as a "subject."

. . . In cases such as this, where subject's background appears to be unduly obscure, it should be clearly understood that no completely satisfactory results can be expected from an investigation limited in scope or time. Within the time allotted it has proved impossible to trace subject's family status or secure concrete proof to establish subject's present character.

It was found that subject did in fact attend the Immaculate Heart Academy of Baltimore, Md., from 1969 to 1977, but faculty and employees of this institute, which is reputed to serve partly as an orphanage besides caring for a certain number of illegitimate offspring of Roman Catholic descent, refused to cooperate in revealing any additional information. Subject left Baltimore and arrived in New York City on June 19, 1977, resided for two weeks at the Betsy Ross Hotel for Women and obtained employment with the Ainslee Agency as a photographic model. Office and Social Security records admit no next of kin and quote Baltimore, April 16, 1959, as subject's place and date of birth. A check of civic records appears to indicate that these data are incorrect, or that subject's name was changed upon her entrance at Immaculate Heart Academy for the exact purpose of screening her real ancestry.

Subject moved into a modest single-room apartment at 4814 Oxford Towers and achieved a measure of professional prominence. Her income is said to have varied between $300 and $500 per week. Subject was considered by her associates to be of a somewhat retiring and straitlaced disposition until November 1977, when she began to appear on a number of social occasions in the company of Alfredo Vanni, Metropolitan Opera baritone and motion picture star, who resided at the time at 55 Central Park South. It was generally assumed by subject's associates that the couple were on intimate terms, and this probability was a matter of speculation in several Broadway newspaper columns at the time in view of Vanni's long-established and colorful reputation for gallantry. However, the affair was conducted with a certain discretion, and at short notice it has not been found possible to discover evidence of any value.

On February 12, 1979, Vanni returned to Hollywood where he is under contract to Globe International Pictures, Inc. Subject secured a release from her contract with the Ainslee Agency on February 15, stating that she wished to become a free-lance model on the West Coast. She arrived in Los Angeles on March 2, and has since resided in a duplex apartment at Sunset Castle, 9880 Dumont Avenue, Beverly Hills. Subject is considered a successful model, but local fees are substantially lower than in the East, and her earnings here are estimated to average less than $250 per week. Subject's rent alone amounts to $600 per month. She is still frequently observed in Vanni's company at fashionable restaurants, and she is known to have been among his guests on several occasions at his San Fernando Valley estate, but Sunset Castle employees claim that he has never been known to visit her apartment, although subject entertains there and appears to enjoy a normal social life. She is understood to appreciate music and owns a fair-sized record library. She does not appear to be actively interested in a motion picture career; however, a routine screen test was made at Globe International on August 21, presumably upon Vanni's suggestion, which test is said to have proved disappointing to talent executives concerned.

Subject continues to display a quiet and reserved personality and to exercise more than average discretion in behavior. It is considered highly probable that her relations with Mr. Vanni amount to more than ordinary friendship, and that a financial arrangement is involved. Further investigation over a period of time is likely to succeed in uncovering conclusive evidence in support of this appraisal. . . .

I read all these fine, cagey words and frowned at them for no special reason, and glanced at Mr. Walter Hitchcock's disapproving scowl. I couldn't see what was so confidential about a middle-aged opera singer paying the rent for his girl friend. Alfredo Vanni could afford a whole seraglio, and probably did.

"Where do you come in, sir?"

The scowl deepened; the gray mustache actually twitched with indignation. He did not want to tell me. He wasn't exactly ashamed of it, or embarrassed by any means. He was just irked about the deal, like a man in a hurry who breaks a shoe-lace.

"That damfool son of mine wants to marry the woman," he said gruffly.

His son! I kept my face straight with an effort. The bold paisley scarf, the pale, emotional, furious eyes, the arrogant private-school accent cracking hysterically on a dirty word. *Something wrong, Mr. Stuart?* No, the sleeping-pill treatment would not be indicated there. Or the visit from the two big, solemn-faced characters with the unctuous manner—"Lady, don't you think this town gets kind of dull after a spell? How's about a nice little trip to South America?" Or even the summons to a stuffy corporation lawyer's office, the rustle of parchment foolscap, the five-figure check. None of those. Not with a headstrong, spoiled, excitable young punk involved, who out of sheer resentment might decide to blow off the roof.

What it would take would be something along the lines of a slightly shopworn Lothario, suitably equipped with a reasonably handsome body and countenance, halfway acceptable social manners and conveniently amputated conscience. One who could be quickly dressed up in some sort of professional glamour, rushed onstage to make with a fast seduction routine and remove the lady to a safe and distant spot by her own free consent. That would be the only smooth, foolproof way of fixing young Mr. Stuart's little red wagon, all right.

"Does she want him?" I asked, just to pretend an interest.

The snort he gave me questioned my intelligence. "Does a fly want sugar? The boy came to see me last Thursday night. He'd met this doll some time ago and expected me to kick in with the price of the ring. If you knew my son you'd realize I couldn't tell him to go roll a hoop. His next stop with her would've been Vegas, and the tap for an annulment anywhere from a hundred G's up. I told him marriage was great stuff, only not to rush his fences. I said I'd give the doll a job for two weeks, posing for ads at my place in Palm Springs, if he'd promise to stay away from her that long. Then if he was still squirming he could slip her the leash with bells on. He fell for it."

It had taken them just three days to have the detective agency tie a tag on her and cast around for a likely-looking fancy man, the kind who would either play ball or wake up on a vacant lot without a face—such as, for instance, me. They'd never have made it with one of their own trained gorillas; the job demanded too many special qualifications. "Maybe you should've let his mother handle this," I said stupidly.

"You kidding?" He wasn't sure if he should get mad or feel sorry for me. "Listen, Bailey, by the time you're as old as I am, and you've had as many of these chiseling little broads try to take you, you'll know better. I don't even remember what she looked like."

"Sorry, my mistake," I said. "You'll think I'm just wasting my chips, Mr. Hitchcock, but the truth is, I can't seem to figure the deal. Why don't you simply ask Vanni to keep his pigeons in the roost?"

"The customer is always right."

"Sir?"

Now they were both of them sneering at me. "Maybe you are not so smart," Steve Kovacs said unpleasantly. "Meester Vanni iss one beeg spender, got many friends already. *Basta*. We do not mess with Meester Vanni. Iss bad for beezness."

"Okay," I said. "I just wanted to know. You gentlemen must have a lot of faith in me. I'm supposed to walk in there and make this young lady forget about a big-spending baritone *and* a possible marriage to fifty million dollars. All she gets out of forgetting is a trip to Bermuda with a joker like me. I'll need a correspondence course in hypnotism, ten easy lessons."

The Big Fellow just shrugged. Kovacs came up with one more folded piece of paper from his breast pocket and dropped it in my lap. It was a tear-out sheet from *Cosmopolitan*, a cigarette ad in full color featuring a slim brunette in riding clothes standing beside a palomino pony. She looked poised, cool, young and not especially attractive, but she did have that peculiar quality women call chic.

She also was, quite unmistakably, as black as Diana Ross.

The yellow rubber duck in the pool bobbed gently up and down, swung around with the breeze and showed me his tail. I bared my teeth at him. They had passed me the dice, faded me the house limit and expected me to shoot. They had probably cooked up something in case I threw snake eyes, but they'd pay off all right on a natural. *She is understood to appreciate music....*

"I'll need some money anyway," I said.

4

PALM SPRINGS AND MONEY is like ham and eggs. Palm Springs has everything—the sun, the mountains and the desert, the low-roofed, air-conditioned Spanish villas and the swanky dude ranches, the haughtily exclusive country clubs. It has the Indians, the mineral prospectors and the cowpunchers, the big excursion buses full of Boy Scouts, and it has the movie stars, the playgirls and the crooks from every corner of the earth. From Hollywood it is a trip of one hundred miles due east. The Ford, minus one fender, made it in two hours that Monday night.

A battered old car may be an affectation or a sentimental attachment, but a wolf must look like a gentleman. I had three hundred dollars' worth of light gray sharkskin gabardine on my back and a good secondhand suitcase full of brand-new play clothes in the trunk. I'd had a haircut and a shampoo and a manicure. I'd got my wristwatch out of hock and bought myself a handsome pin-seal wallet and a pair of woven-leather moccasins that had a lot of quiet class, bearing in mind that there are women who will judge a man almost entirely by his shoes.

I'd paid my bill at the motel, picked up my

shaving gear, and at about six-thirty pushed the
buzzer button under the neatly mounted strip of
visiting card with *Marion Faraday* on it in
carefully engraved six point Old English. That
was my first mistake right there.

"Yes, what is it...? Oh, no! Rick, I don't
believe it!"

"Take it easy, kid. It's only me."

"But I didn't recognize you! Darling, you look
positively *glamorous*!"

"Just sniff the air. Some faint odor of brim-
stone."

"Come on in, quick, before that slinky witch
across the hall sees you. Mmm! Yum-yum-
yum.... Hold me tight, Ricky—nice Ricky! You
got the job."

"Yeah, I got it."

"We'll have to celebrate. A dry martini, please,
Jeeves. Veddy, veddy dry. I'm fixing supper for
us, but it won't burn. We can have a drink, and
sit on the couch, and neck, and you can tell me
all about it."

I managed to grin at her warily. She had on
something long and pink and lacy with a lot of
ruffles that she called a hostess gown, and her
blond shoulder-length hair was fluffy from the
brush. Her wide hazel eyes were dancing with
excitement. From nine to five, five days a week,
they were more likely to stand firmly at attention, and her office wardrobe consisted of nothing but plain and severely cut tweed suits. She
had the kind of figure that looks trim and interesting in a really expensive girdle. She was a
great girl, Marion: smart, willful, loyal, pos-

sessive, warmhearted, hot-tempered, self-confident. Virtuous, even, in her fashion; an uncomplicated kind of virtue that held that nothing was bad if you felt sorry for the guy and he was considerate about things, and properly appreciative.

"One dry martini coming up," I said.

A drink, a couch and a blonde make up a fairly sound combination when a man has time on his hands and nothing on his mind. I wasn't even sure about being a man. I kept my back against the wall to create an illusion of owning some sort of a spine. Nice Ricky, nice cocktail.

"Darling, do sit down. Tell me."

"Not much to tell. I can't stay long."

"Why not?"

"This job. I'm flying East tonight. I've got to line up fourteen sidemen, see about rehearsals, auditions, transportation, everything. It's a pretty big deal, such as like setting fire to a madhouse."

"Oh, Rick, that's *wonderful*! Where do you open?"

"Miami Beach."

"When?"

"Next month, the twenty-first."

"But that's five weeks from now. You've always told me you could get a band shaped up in three."

"Sure, three days. Three bottles of gin. Three doodlesack pipers."

She frowned at me. "Rick, what about the union?"

"They're taking care of that."

"Hitchcock Hotels? Did you have to explain?"

"No, they knew all about me."

"That's the Marlborough Plaza in Miami Beach, isn't it? We ran some copy for it in *Holiday* last year." She nibbled on her olive thoughtfully. "Rick, I'm going with you."

"Hey, just a minute now. You know you can't do that."

"Yes, I can. I'll call Mr. Jeffries right now and get a leave of absence. You'll need help, darling. I'll be very useful to you."

She was already reaching for the phone. I crossed the room in a hurry and took the receiver away from her. "Don't be silly. You don't know a thing about the music business. I'll have to move fast to get organized. This means a lot to me."

"Rick, listen—"

"No dice. You've got a good job where you are. This deal may easily turn into a flop."

"Not if I'm around to keep you out of mischief. Darling, don't you think I realize this is your one big chance? That's why you need me with you to look after you and, well, you know. . . ."

"No, thanks. This time I'll look after myself."

She stared at me for a long time. "Which flight are you taking?"

"How's that again? Oh, the plane. I don't know. They told me to report to T.W.A. at nine."

"I see."

"I'll have to get a move on pretty soon."

"Yes, of course," she agreed distantly. "When will I see you again?"

"Three, four months, maybe. As soon as I'm settled and back in the chips."

Her empty cocktail glass came whizzing. I ducked and heard it shatter against the baseboard behind me. She was suddenly pale and trembling, and her eyes blazed wide with anger. "Oh, fine," I said. "Now what was that in aid of?"

"You're lying to me again. I can't stand it when you lie to me."

"I don't know what you're talking about. This isn't a brush-off, sweetheart, not if I can help it."

"Oh, you'll be back all right," she said nastily. "And it won't be in anything like three months. You'll be back tomorrow, or maybe next week, because you're not going anywhere, and it won't take you long to let those few hundred dollars you won today go down the drain once more. Then you'll be forced to come around scrounging for a meal again, and laundry money, and to have me mend the holes in your socks. And I'm just silly enough to oblige. But you might at least wipe that injured look off your face."

"Sorry. I guess I'm not much good at pretending. Or at anything else for that matter."

She swung off the couch in a flash of long, seductively muscular legs and grabbed my shoulders, shaking me with everything she had. "Will you listen to me! Rick, for God's sake, will you *please* stop knocking yourself! You *are* good at things, you are so. You're talented, and handsome, and clever in many ways, and most of the time we've known each other you've been good for me. If only you'd stop beating your head against the wall and get this—this damned *kink* out of your system, you could.... Darling, let's drive down to Yuma or to Mexico tonight and get it over with!"

"What?"

"Yes, I'm asking you. I never thought I could do it, but there it is."

"How many drinks did you have by yourself just now?" I asked her stupidly.

"Rick, I'm serious. Marriage would be so right for you—for both of us. I could make you keep regular hours, and get a job, and feel responsible for me and all that stuff. You remember what the psychiatrist told you."

"Oh, him. He didn't tell me to get married."

"He told you only a woman could set you straight."

"It has been tried. The patient seems to have developed a certain immunity."

We looked at each other for a while in one of those sober, calculating silences that never get anywhere, and then she smiled at me archly and punched me lightly on the chin, like a man. "You'll learn, darling. I'll get my hooks into you yet. Hungry?"

"Yes, but I'd better go now."

"Calf's liver and onions, smothered, the way you like them."

I sighed and shook my head. "You don't understand. I really meant it, about leaving town for a few months."

"Oh, Rick, don't let's start that all over again. How much *did* you win today?"

Her lips were pouting at me, demanding attention, not more than inches away. I kissed them

gently and almost ran out of the apartment.
Something crashed against the door on the instant it slammed behind me, probably an ashtray.
I hurried down one flight of steps and rang for
the elevator on the floor below. The cocky little
Filipino operator winked at me. "Gee, you look
pretty good today, Mr. Bailey."

"Thanks, Pablo. So do you."

He chuckled and went through the business of
spitting on his hand and rattling his fist from the
elbow. "Little game we got us up tonight down
janitor's basement. Yes, sir, yes, sir. Come on,
baby, not so close, papa needs quinine, the bitter
dose. You wanna see some fun, Mr. Bailey?"

The spot I was in, and still I had to brace myself
and dig nails into my palms.

"Not tonight, kid. Got a date."

"Yes, sir, yes, sir." He sucked air through his
teeth in an almost perfect imitation of the dice
scampering across a concrete floor. "Forty-
five," he chortled. "Baby, what shot Jesse
James? A forty-five! This ain't your floor, is it,
Mr. Bailey?"

"Step on it, you lousy creep," I growled.

"Yes, sir, yes, sir."

Outside, the Ford's starter balked at me three
times before I could get rolling down to Wilshire
Boulevard and out into the stream of headlights
traveling east.

5

On Tuesday morning the strident twitter of a mockingbird making like a lark outside my window pushed me back to the surface. Sunlight lay in a crisp, intricate pattern on the bedroom's elegant powder-blue carpet, the furniture's starched, expensive chintz, but the air was still cool and filled with the clean sibilance of sprinklers whirling on the lawn. My head felt heavy from thinking long, involved, unpleasant thoughts through most of the night. I shook the gravel out of it under the shower, shaved with more than my customary fastidiousness and climbed into a T-shirt and a pair of shorts.

Breakfast meant quite a little walk. The Hacienda del Sol covered something like twenty acres, an elaborately landscaped park surrounded on three sides by towering orchards of date palms. Eastward the desert bloomed in yellow, white and royal-purple splendor of verbena, sunflower and primrose welcoming the spring; westward the formidable San Jacinto range soared to its vast escarpment of a thousand pastel colors topped by the bright glitter of eternal snow.

Crushed oystershell paved the network of footpaths laid out in a complicated geometrical

design across the hotel park, connecting each in-
dividual bungalow with all the others and with a
sprawling pavilion of brick and glazed adobe
where dining room and bar, reception hall and
ballroom were combined under one roof. The
night before a sleepy Mexican porter had
wheeled my suitcase on a chromium-plated bag-
gage dolly down the path from the courtyard,
and the park had been dark, cold and silent. Now
it was basking in the sun as quietly as a high-class
cemetery. There were no children playing under
the olive trees; not a single dog disturbed the
peace of the carefully manicured greensward.

In the dining room a handful of guests were
addressing themselves to a choice of seven
meats, six eggs, a dozen breads and cereals and
the usual fruits and beverages. The paunchy,
frock-coated headwaiter favored me with a stare
so blandly dubious as to make me wonder if he
knew exactly what I was about. Then it occurred
to me he was more likely to have noticed that I
happened to be the only living specimen in the
room who was obviously under sixty years old.
The Hacienda del Sol, it seemed, did not
specialize in catering to the family trade, and
presumably charged rates in accordance with
that policy.

I took a leisurely breakfast aboard without
much appetite, watching a few more elderly
ladies and gentlemen drift into and out of the
establishment. By eleven o'clock there did not
seem to be much point in stalling any longer. In
the park even the sprinkler system had been
turned off; the only sign of human life was an

occasional recumbent form on the steamer chairs set out on each bungalow patio under the dripping bougainvillea. A painted wooden arrow directed me to the swimming pool. That took another nice little walk, beyond the main compound through a strip of date garden, past the tennis courts into a sort of bower surrounded by tangerine trees, neatly trimmed and in full bearing. The bathhouse was glass brick and structural aluminum, the pool a gleaming oval of turquoise; there were rubber mattresses and air-foam cushions and huge, gaily striped beach umbrellas by the score.

The sole beneficiary of all these creature comforts appeared to be a short chunky man in prim white ducks and sneakers who sat on the Ping-Pong table moodily surveying the scenery and expertly juggling four of the little celluloid balls. He had the square, heavy features, the leathery tan, the stiff, grizzled hair of an old professional athlete; his chunkiness was visibly all muscle. He saw me and jumped to the deck in a hurry. There was nothing dubious about his particular brand of surprise.

"*Good* morning, sir. Were you looking for me?"

I squeezed out a grin for him. "Don't know myself what I'm looking for," I said, and told him my name.

"Joe Cornero," he said. "Director of recreation." He made it sound as if formality embarrassed him, and his handshake gave me a wince. "Maybe you want to sharpen up your tennis game a bit?"

"It's a thought. You get many customers here?"

He squinted at me, carefully appraising. "You don't need no appointment, that's for sure," he admitted. "Staying long, Mr. Bailey?"

"Don't know yet. Couple of weeks, maybe."

He kept studying me with that funny expression of trying to place me. Then he surprised the stuffing out of me by saying, "Roseland Palace, in Atlantic City."

"Quite a memory," I said uneasily.

"Shucks, that was nothing, Mr. Bailey. You don't remember me, on account of you were up there on that stage, and I was down in the hall most every night with a couple of dolls off the beach. Lifeguard captain—you know how it is. Come to think of it, I never did catch up with you again in all these years. You opening in town here soon?"

"Just resting."

"You sure picked the place."

"Seems like as if. No music here, is there?"

"We get us up a square dance every now 'n' then," he grinned. "One o' them hillbilly outfits. You wouldn't care so much about that."

"Got a piano somewhere?" I asked him, suddenly worried.

He pointed at the bathhouse. "Right in there. Moved it from the ballroom—too many amachoors worked out on it, too many kicks from the other guests. This joint ain't exactly jumping," he added dryly.

I went in to see, and he tagged along behind me. The bathhouse faced the pool with a sliding patio door. There was a coconut rug, a small bamboo bar and some modernized log cabin furniture. The piano was a Blüthner concert grand, extra fancy style, a special nightclub job laid in with burnished mother-of-pearl. Its presence created a sort of slapdash baroque effect, like having a stand of armor in your living room.

I flipped back the cover and struck a few keys at random. They had kept it tuned, and the tone was surprisingly resonant, clean and sharp in the distaff, rich and sonorous in the bass. An electrical player attachment lurked below the keyboard with a roll hooked up. I looked at it and bared a tooth; it was the "Poet and Peasant" overture.

"Go ahead and play, Mr. Bailey," Joe Cornero said. "This is too far away for them old battle-axes to complain."

I ran a few scales, then tackled a Chopin étude. The difference from Marion's little spinet was something like driving a diesel truck compared to a horse and buggy. My fingers were stiff and wanted to stumble all over the place. Cornero hung across the bar, listening politely, his corrugated-leather face expressionless. I switched to Brahms's "Hungarian Dance" and he perked up a bit.

"Not so many of you fellows know something about that longhair stuff," he offered.

"Well, don't let me fool you. I can't play this thing, either. All I ever learned was how to fake around."

"Sounds okay to me, Mr. Bailey." He was knitting his eyebrows, wondering if he had a wise guy on his hands after all. I dropped the classics like a hot potato and gave him a couple of riffs

out of "Maple Leaf Rag," which used to be one
of our feature numbers. That was more like it, in
his book. He broke into a smile and started snapping his fingers.

"Now you're cooking for sure, Mr. Bailey. All
we need now is a couple of dolls off that beach in
Atlantic City."

"You're the director of recreation here," I
said. "Where's this merchandise you're keeping
under the counter for special customers?"

"Shucks, Palm Springs is bustin' at the seams
with dolls," he solemnly assured me. "They
come in any size, shape and color, anytime
you're ready, Mr. Bailey. It's just the management don't like it if you bring 'em in. They got
this rule here that says all facilities for the con-
venience of registered guests only. You know
how it is."

"Maybe we'd better check the register," I said.

"I'm way ahead of you there, Mr. Bailey. All
we got just now is them old battle-axes."

"That was no battle-ax I saw at breakfast,
Joe."

He gave me a puzzled frown. "Must have been
Mrs. Jones. She's married—he's with her.
They're older than you and they keep to themselves. Then there's Miss Ryan, but she don't eat
breakfast."

"Trying to reduce?"

"Uh-uh. Nothing like that." I really had him
building up the pot now. "She's got a figure all
right. Reckon she aims to hang on to it. One o'
them snooty Hollywood models." He saw my
wink and shook his head to warn me off the

track. "She's been here for a couple days, waiting for this photographer to show. They're gonna take some pictures for an ad. Don't waste your time, Mr. Bailey."

"Why?"

"Models," he scoffed. "They're worse than actresses. All they ever care about is what they can see in the mirror. All a man's supposed to do is look and pay the bills, and that's for sure. This Miss Ryan, she's black, but she's no different. She sits around all day, reading them fashion magazines. She's already got a mink coat, if you follow me."

We grinned at each other and the phone started ringing. Somebody wanted him to arrange for a couple of horses after lunch. Gentle ones. He said he'd see about it right away and hurried off to the corrals, holding up a finger at me in admonishing salute. I waited until he was out of earshot and then got down to business on the Blüthner, exercising systematically, limbering up my wrists, going back over a lot of territory that was still familiar but needed to be revisited.

I stayed with it all afternoon, skipping lunch. Joe Cornero didn't show up anymore and the pool remained deserted. The thermometer in the bathhouse climbed to ninety. I found a stack of terry towels in a closet. I used one to sit on, one to dry my face, and one to wipe the keyboard and my hands about every other five minutes. Around 6:00 P.M. the sun ducked suddenly behind the mountains and a breeze came whistling through the date palms. It got cold and dark so fast I had to wrap myself in another towel and take off for my bungalow at a run or risk catching pneumonia. By that time the Blüthner was ready to sit up and beg.

At seven, freshly cleaned and pressed, I strolled into the bar, a cavernous affair in terracotta tile. The open fireplace had a stack of pine logs roaring away, and on the wall above it an eighteenth-century caballero bestrode his fiery black stallion in life-size four-color tile mosaic. Behind the counter three harassed white-coated Mexicans toiled on the cocktail assembly line; the room was rank with cigarette smoke and buzzing with the dinner crowd. A straw-blond youth in fancy cowpuncher duds drifted among the tables, strumming his guitar and dispensing the usual sagebrush cantos in a bland, sugary tenor.

I managed a toehold on the rail and a Scotch in my hand and looked the situation over. It occurred to me then, a trifle belatedly, that Mr. Walter Hitchcock had thoughtfully fixed the wheel for me. The Hacienda del Sol afforded exactly the right background for casual romance, but its masculine patrons were unlikely to supply me with serious competition.

The woman next to me threw her head back and laughed out loud. She had the kind of laugh you'd expect to hear in a zoo, if they had a bar for hyenas. Her sudden movement jiggled my elbow and spilled some of my drink. She finished laughing, noticed me and made a fuzzy double take.

"Sorry," I said, like a little gentleman.

"Oooh, nice mans! Burt, lookie here. See the nice mans?"

The fellow with her inspected me dutifully. He was a skinny sawed-off runt in a dinner jacket, whose few remaining wispy locks of gray clung stubbornly to an otherwise pink and perfectly egg-shaped skull. "Now, angel face..." he protested weakly, pursing his lips at me in anxious deprecation.

"Buy nice mans another drink," the woman ordered him. She hung on to me with one of those I-could-eat-you-with-a-little-silver-teaspoon looks. She was a blonde who could still make the grade, but only just; there is a point at which they don't fool around with slacks or a bathing suit anymore, but in a white lamé dress under dim artificial light they can still knock you dead. The small, plump, freckled hand she laid demurely on my sleeve sported a wedding ring with several good-sized square-cut diamonds.

The skinny fellow bought a drink and offered me three bony little fingers. I remembered Joe Cornero's briefing and caught the name. *She's married—he's with her....* "Pleased to meet you, Mr. Jones. Where you people from?"

"Now, angel face...."

That was all right. I'd been in bars before. I could have kept it up for hours, waltzing them around and no harm done. I bought another drink, and that made us Rick, Burt and Rita. They would have made me wonder, if I hadn't had my own straight to fill. The southern accent was an obvious phony, and somehow the guy seemed worried about bigger problems than his wife's making a pass at me.

Then, clear across the room, I spotted Lorna Ryan.

She had a table over by the wall, half-hidden by a pillar, and she sat very straight, sipping her sherry and disinterestedly watching the cowboy singer serenading her. She looked terribly sure of herself, as if she owned the joint with everybody in it and his Uncle Harry. Her silk shirt dress was the kind that doesn't seem like much and takes a steady hand when you write the check for it. I disliked her on sight, a whole hell of a lot.

There was another, older woman with her who was showing me her back and a somewhat disorderly mop of gray hair. I bit my lip; the Joneses had caught on and were staring, Bert with something of a twisted grin, Rita squinting in a way that was either malicious or myopic, or both.

"You two seem to know the young lady," I said.

Burt started guiltily and turned back to the bar in a hurry. Rita gave me a venomous little chuckle.

"Let up on the throttle, handsome," she admonished me. "You're burning out a bearing." She didn't sound tight or southern anymore.

"Now, angel face. . . ."

The dinner gong clanged its merrily insistent summons.

6

IN THE CARD ROOM four early diners were already clustered around a bridge table when I walked in with my hatches battened down over a load of lobster cocktail and breast of guinea hen Provençal. There was quite an argument going on over the correct penalty for a revoke. I kibitzed awhile until somebody mentioned they were playing for all of a nickel a hundred.

Just looking at the cards made me restless and set up the old stinging in my veins. Joe Cornero came in, plainly uncomfortable in a stiff black tie, and proceeded to distribute backgammon and cribbage boards. He cocked an eyebrow at me when I asked him.

"Sure, there's some of 'em around," he told me. "I'd try the Tahquitz Casino if I was you, Mr. Bailey. Turn left onto the country road at Onowanda Park, about two miles. I hear they're middling straight."

"Give me a deck," I said. "Maybe I can work this off."

He watched me closely while I dealt a hand of solitaire. Sometimes it helped me get back on the beam, because of its peculiar, almost unlimited capacity for taxing the so-called human brain.

This was one time I needed to stay on the beam. The cards felt crisp and slippery; they were the varnished kind and they kept skidding through my shaky fingers. At last I had the layout and began to study it, testing various preliminary plays and combinations in my mind before making a move. The stinging subsided a little and my hands relaxed.

A woman's voice spoke up behind my shoulder, sharply inquisitive. "What in the world is that you're keeping from us fellow morons there, my friend?"

I glanced at her and got up in a hurry. She was in her fifties, though not quite as gray and disarranged as I had thought. There was a lean mannishness about her, and that peculiar sort of intellectual detachment you can catch in pictures of nuclear scientists. She wasn't by any means the gregarious social meddler type, but she certainly had no intention of allowing the conventions to interfere with her curiosity. Beside her Lorna Ryan looked on, apparently amused with her.

Joe Cornero cleared his throat, hastily muttered introductions and tiptoed away. The lady's name seemed to be Garand; I wondered if she had invented the automatic rifle, but I wasn't in the mood to quarrel with my luck just then. There were bows to be made and chairs to be offered and the usual meaningless platitudes to be exchanged. But she really wanted to know about the cards.

"Lorna thought you were telling your own fortune...." She looked at me, brightly expectant.

I glanced at the girl in the shirt dress, who was smiling rather vaguely. She had blue eyes, the dark, translucent blue of an expensive sapphire. Their hue contrasted interestingly with the light chocolate of her complexion and the gleaming sable of her fashionably cut and disciplined short locks.

"Must be the Gypsy in me that's showing," I said. "This game is called King's Cross, and it's the only form of idiot's delight I know of that requires serious mental exercise. You can win in theory almost every time, but most layouts are so difficult that it takes a computer to solve them. On the other hand you can just go ahead and play it blind, without any effort at all. But the odds are a million to one you'll wind up in a mess."

"It sounds fascinating," Mrs. Garand said cheerfully. "Which system do you practice, or is that a fair question?"

I realized then that she was more interested in people than in games, and started digging in fast.

"It's not much fun unless you try to stay with it. I suppose that goes for almost anything, from beer to religion. In this case you arrange the deck in four straight horizontal rows of thirteen cards, faceup. You remove the aces and lay them aside, which leaves forty-eight cards and four holes. Now the idea is to work out a tableau in which everything runs in sequence, from deuces to the kings, from left to right: clubs in the top row, diamonds in the second, hearts and spades. Looks easy, but it's not."

The Ryan girl opened her purse and took out a thin beveled-gold case, the kind that holds half a dozen cigarettes, a compact and mirror. She posed gracefully toward the light, inspecting the cool, disdainful sweep of her lashes, repairing a tiny blemish in her makeup. I still resented her, but I had to admit to myself that she was attractive, after all; the way some orchids are attractive simply because of an unusual pattern of designs and color shade. Her cheekbones were too high, and the cheeks almost hollow, the slim, pointed ears too large, the sulky, darkly carmined mouth too small, yet somehow in their combination they achieved an effect, a quality of sensitivity, a dry-martini sort of charm. She suddenly became aware that I was watching her and returned my stare with one of almost childish composure.

Mrs. Garand's glance flickered between us roguishly.

"But why King's Cross?" she pressed me. "How are you supposed to move?"

I forced a grin and said, "You asked for it, madam. Don't put the blame on me after the orderlies from the sanatorium call around for you with an ambulance. You're supposed to move cards from the tableau into these holes left by the aces. That creates new holes, of course, which you must fill in turn, until at last you get the layout straight in sequence, always from left to right, with the kings at the end. Each hole may be filled only with the next highest card, counting from the left in the same row. For example, here's the ten of spades with a hole on the right behind it. I can fill that only with the jack of spades, but I'm not going to do it. Not now."

"Why not?"

"Because the jack of spades now lies behind the four of diamonds, and because the five of diamonds, which is the only card to plug *that* hole, lies blocked behind the king of clubs. King's Cross, you see: no card will go into a hole behind a king—you've got to move in such a way that the four kings don't cross you up. They can be moved themselves, of course, behind their queens, until you finally work them over to the end of their row. Sometimes it's necessary to create a temporary block or two, if you can foresee where later moves will clear those blocks again. But each move with all its alternates and permutations must be carefully planned in advance, or else in no time you're in trouble with nothing but holes behind the kings. It sounds silly, but in fact it's almost unbelievably complicated."

She followed me all right, and she was even mildly interested, but when I tried out a few moves to illustrate she quickly reverted to type. "Are you an artist or a musician, Mr. Bailey?"

"Well, lackaday," I said, uncomfortably startled. "What goes on here? Do I really look emotionally unstable?"

She did not even smile. The Ryan girl selected a cigarette and waited for me to come up with a match. "Eve has a hobby," she told me. "She's been watching your hands." Her voice was low, slightly husky and impersonal to the point of indifference.

"Gamblers have hands like these," I suggested, leaning recklessly into the wind.

Mrs. Garand shook her head; her beady little eyes were as bright as a sparrow's. "Steadier," she said. "Much steadier. If they afford this place. And you're too careful about your appearance for an artist, so you must be a musician. A good one."

"Now you're just being kind. Who's a good musician? There's Heifetz, Rubinstein, Giulini. All I do is go through the motions. Like that cowhand in the bar with his guitar."

The girl crushed her half-smoked cigarette in the ashtray.

"I think he's perfectly awful," she said without any particular emphasis.

7

On Wednesday morning after breakfast I tried the gift shop in the lobby. They had just the thing: a hand-embroidered blue chiffon scarf, extra sheer and of a shade that served to match her eyes. It was expensive enough for her to wear, and not presumptuous enough that she'd have to return it. I put a king of diamonds with it in the box to supply the light touch, and had them deliver it to her bungalow.

The Joneses were splashing around in the pool and ignoring me. I slapped on some suntan oil and loafed the morning away on a deck chair, sweating out the deal. It was hotter than a steak fry in hell, and the heavy cloying scent of the tangerine trees became suffocating as the day dragged on.

By noon I was in a fine case of physical indolence and mental agitation. The swimmers walked by on their way to lunch, Burt with a scowl, Rita with a sidelong glance. Joe Cornero turned up soon after, bullied me into a Ping-Pong game, beat the stuffing out of me in three fast sets and forced a quart of ice water and some salt tablets from the bathhouse bar into my system.

I was fast asleep when the diving board

screamed and the pool exploded in my ears. For several seconds there was nothing but the sun striking swiftly widening rings of fire off the surface, and then Lorna Ryan bobbed up at the other end and easily swung herself back to the tile walk. She waved at me quite casually and ran for the tower again. On the high board she posed against the sky, rather longer and more ostentatiously than the average diver, I thought. Her white French satin bikini, laced together with deceptive flimsiness, did not appear especially daring or seductive; somehow bikinis seem natural on these very sylphlike, long-limbed, high-breasted bodies that have learned to control themselves, never to be caught off guard or in so much as an instant's gawkiness. I didn't even flatter myself that the show was for my benefit— she was merely working her trade, not deliberately but as a matter of unconscious policy. The board groaned once more and she jackknifed expertly in midair, flashing into the water like a seal.

This time she came up less than two feet away from me, smiling mischievously.

"Hi! Did we disturb you?"

I glanced across to where Mrs. Garand was sitting in the shade, reading a brightly jacketed novel. "Hi, yourself," I said. "Do I look disturbed?"

"I don't know you well enough to tell," she countered, and again there was about her this disconcerting simplicity, this cool childishness, as if she were totally lacking in the feminine arts and wiles. "Thank you for my pretty blue scarf," she added gravely. It was the same tone, the same expression that would have applied if I'd offered her a bite out of my apple after school, because it was her birthday.

"Flowers would have been more suitable," I said, a bit uneasily. "But not with a whole desertful of them around, and I wanted to find something for you. Are you ladies old friends?"

"Oh, no. We've just met. Don't you know about Eve?"

"Should I?"

"She's a famous writer. Books and things."

"Oh...."

"She's awfully smart. I like her, don't you?"

"A writer," I said. "Nice work. How about you? Haven't I seen you in pictures?" Her laugh was completely unstilted, almost hearty, and very much at my expense. "What's funny?"

"People are always asking me that. You've seen me in lots of pictures. Billboards, fashion ads, magazine covers. I used to be an Ainslee model, before I got movie-struck and flew out from New York last year."

"No dice, you mean?" I asked her, quasi-incredulous.

"Not a chance," she confessed gaily. "I'm a terrible actress. Can't you tell?"

I stared at her, holding back my frown with an effort, forcibly reminding myself that she was almost twenty-one and had been around, the way Spectacular Bid had been around Santa Anita. Walter Hitchcock's voice rasped in my ear. *You're supposed to get this bim out of my hair....*

"Race you across the pool?" I offered, and took a flying header off my chair into the water.

She outdistanced me easily, and I am not a weak swimmer. I wasn't worried about that so much, because it's a fact that nowadays for quick success in any courtship, phony or otherwise, there's a distinct advantage to you in allowing the female of the species to enjoy immediate superiority in something or other, so she'll be the more impressed with your real accomplishments as they come to light. I let her enjoy hers, playing the usual games. Then after half an hour or so I pulled out and sprawled on one of the rubber mattresses, pretending to be winded.

"Got to take it easy. Little bit out of condition."

She sat on the lawn beside me, hugging her knees and soberly watching me. "There's nothing wrong with you, is there?"

"Why do you say that?"

"I don't know. The way you sounded."

"Well, not anymore."

"I shouldn't have asked."

"Sure, that's all right. No secret. I go out of circulation for a while, from time to time. Delayed C.F."

"What's that?"

"Combat fatigue. Vietnam, ten years ago. It can catch up with you. Like getting scared a week after an accident."

"Oh, I'm so sorry."

"Don't be. I was lucky."

"But ten years. . . ."

I shrugged it off. The sympathy angle had to be

worked, but I didn't much care for the taste it left in my mouth. "It comes and goes. Time out of mind. I'm in good shape again. Going East in a couple of weeks, start a new band, get back on the ball. We're opening in Bermuda next month."

"Oh, you're a bandleader." She was politely interested now, no more.

"Hotels and the old-fashioned style of ballrooms. Cruise liners, sometimes, and private parties. Very square, but it's a living. At your age I don't imagine that's the kind of music you get into very much."

She looked at me wide-eyed, puzzled with me. "You can't mean I'm supposed to be a rock fan just because I'm young."

"I guess I did. Maybe because I used to worry a lot about rock. There's such a bunch of bread in it, and some of it is pretty tricky stuff. But there were reasons why it didn't work for me to go that route. What sort of music do you like?"

"I don't know." The question seemed to bother her. "Do you mean mood music, when you're alone and you put something on the stereo, just to sit and listen? I've almost worn out my Gershwin albums that way."

"You talked me into it," I said cheerfully, jumping to my feet and dragging her with me, pouring on the eager animation. It was the wrong approach by a mile, but the deal was getting on my nerves. I needed a peek at my hole card, and I needed it fast.

Across the pool Eve Garand smiled upon us benignly and wiggled her fingers, like mama super-

vising the kiddies at play. In the bathhouse the
Blüthner shimmered in all its garish carnival
splendor; the nacreous panelwork appeared
almost grotesque. Lorna shrank from it as if she
expected it to growl at her.

"Oh, golly. Just what the psychiatrist
ordered!"

I laughed hollowly and spread a towel on the
bench, but she wouldn't sit down. She stood just
inside the door, huddled in her beach wrap,
watching the proceedings with an expression of
helpless dismay.

"Me and Oscar Levant," I said, flipping the
cover off the keyboard and striking the opening
clarinet glissando of "Rhapsody in Blue."

For the first few minutes it seemed to come off
pretty well. She couldn't have made it easier for
me than by mentioning Gershwin herself, and I
don't play any simplified special arrangement of
the "Rhapsody," either—I do Grofé's full-
orchestra score with all the trimmings, or as
nearly as it can be done by one musician with ten
fingers and two feet. There is a real difference
between a pianist and a man accustomed to con-
ducting from behind the piano, the way they see
and interpret a piece of music. One is preoccupied only with his own instrument, while the
other is so used to dealing with two dozen at a
time that he attempts to transmit them all to his
audience—brasses, woodwinds, strings and per-
cussion—the staccato sting of the muted
trumpet, the velvet moan of the saxophone sex-
tet, the horselaugh of a trombone through the
hat, the massive crescendo of a carefully disci-

plined ensemble moving for the climax. With
all of these I could still hold my own. There
were no embarrassing slips or misfires; my
spadework of the afternoon before duly paid
off its dividends, and the Blüthner responded satisfactorily enough. To an extent and
for a while I even managed to recapture
something of the old, almost forgotten en-
joyment familiar to every performer—that peculiar showman's thrill when someone is watching
and listening, anyone at all who is capable
of applying the palms of both hands to each
other.

But very soon I knew it was no use. I was playing the right notes, in the right combinations,
with commendable technique and with all the
approved display of supposedly effortless
brilliance, and still I might just as well have saved
myself the trouble. Somehow the music sounded
like a demonstration of a shiny new pneumatic
drill on raw concrete. It was rapid, clamorous
and highly efficient; it did the job and proved the
operator's skill and clearly showed him to be interested only in making a sale.

Cold perspiration broke between my shoulder
blades in defiance of the blaze of sunlight stream-
ing in through the big picture window behind my
back. The keyboard suddenly grew slippery and
seemed to recede out of my reach; the flowery
cadenza I was working on dissolved abruptly into
dissonance. I managed something like a short,
hard laugh and dug for a cigarette in the pockets
of my robe.

"Sorry," I said, surprising myself by sounding

casual about it. "All refunds at the box office, please. The maestro is indisposed today."

She hadn't moved an inch from where she was standing, still with her wrap pulled tight around her, as if she was afraid of catching a chill in that heat, but now she removed her cap and shook out her gleaming locks. The gesture is one few girls can accomplish gracefully, but she made it appear like a carefully styled figure from a modern ballet.

"You do have rather nice hands," she observed gravely, regarding me without so much as the hint of a smile.

"My mother's. She was a concert harpist, of all things."

She took a step or two and gingerly touched the Blüthner's glossy panelwork. "You've lost her?" she asked me in a small, quiet voice.

"Oh, yes. In '67, a traffic accident."

"Your father, too?"

"He was killed in action," I said without frowning at her. "In the Battle of the Bulge. I never knew him."

She nodded as if I'd made a point, and it occurred to me that she was actually looking for excuses for my shortcomings. The notion would have embarrassed me beyond speech if I could have afforded the luxury of embarrassment.

"Let's do the town tonight," I offered brusquely. "There's a pretty good show at the Cactus Patch, and you must be tired of the atmosphere in this old ladies' home by now."

"I couldn't possibly."

There was nothing coy or demure about her

refusal, and nothing apologetic. It was a simple statement of fact, the way a carefully brought-up child would decline to accept a piece of candy from a stranger, and it got nicely under my skin.

"Why not?"

"So many reasons. There are some letters I've got to answer, and I'm expecting a telephone call after dinner—"

"Of course," I said, fairly nastily. "You must have a lot of friends."

"Don't you?" She was the very picture of wide-eyed serenity.

I wanted to pick a fight with her so badly, I could taste it, and sometimes you're supposed to get results that way much more quickly than by sticking to routine and playing the gentleman, but the most I managed to deliver was a muttered remark about being fresh out of friends who'd expect me to sit by the phone all evening. All that got me was one gracefully trimmed eyebrow slightly raised.

"This is a business call," she told me coolly.

"I see. But you made it sound as if I were trespassing on private property."

The words seemed to hang resonantly in the air between us as if they were echoing a hundred times off the walls, yet for the effect they had on her she might not even have heard me. "Perhaps later this week," she said, brightly specious. "If I'm still here. Will you excuse me now? I think Eve wants to go and change for dinner."

She walked away from me across the hot blue tiles, calmly unhurried, showing me a quick, conventional smile of dismissal over her shoulder. I stood in the doorway smoking and staring after her for a long time. It was near dusk when I got back to my bungalow, and the vast chorus of the crickets was already trying out for pitch and harmony. I sat on the bed for a while, still in my trunks and robe and with the sweat mucous and clammy on my back. The round, sightless face of the phone on the night table leered at me through the shadows. It took me half an hour and half a dozen false starts before I could pick up the receiver.

From Bel Air, across a hundred and twenty miles of desert and orange groves, came the hoarse Irish bass of the pug in chauffeur's leggings. It recognized me and turned to a faintly derisive familiarity. "Yeah, Bailey...he ain't here. How's that? Nah, they're all out to dinner somewhere. Any message?"

"When do you expect him?" I demanded uncomfortably.

"You're asking me, fella. If he don't wind up at the beach place, he could get in by two or three, but I wouldn't disturb him then if I was you. Something I can do for you?" He waited for me to answer, patiently enough. "Whatsamatter, Jack, you in trouble or something...? Hey, wake up, will ya, what goes?"

"No trouble," I told him wearily at last. "Just tell the boss I think I've got things pretty well under control. I'll call again in a day or two."

"Okay, fella. I'll tell him. That all you want?"

"Yes, that's all."

"Okay, I got it. Take your time, huh? No hurry."

I hung up on this cheerful note and sat brooding some more, bickering with myself. It occurred to me that I might just as well have been consistent and asked him to make that photographer get out of my hair with his stalling act over the phone, to keep the girl lined up for me on the Big Fellow's orders. If it *was* the photographer. I made a noise of disgust and stumbled into the shower, dressed and wandered out to the courtyard where my dusty old Ford huddled meekly in the dark among the Lincoln Continentals and the Cadillacs.

8

THE TAHQUITZ CASINO looked straight all right. It clearly had too much of an investment to protect, and too much invested in protection.

From the road all they gave you were a couple of palm trees, a small purple neon sign and a distinct perspective of the sprawling Western country-club-style brick pavilion at the end of a quarter mile of driveway. From the parking lot you got a showcase view of the glass-enclosed patio bar, discreetly illuminated in low key, something like a high-budget movie set for a dude-ranch comedy under rehearsal, with a sprinkling of extras in resort-type evening dress drifting about. From the gate to the parking lot they had you fenced in, the way cattle are guided to the slaughter pen: on wheels or on foot, you went where they'd laid out a course for you between six-foot-high steel trelliswork screened all over with climbing roses in full bloom. Under the rustic front-door arch a pair of strapping flunkies in gold-embroidered bullfighter jackets and Mexican sombreros functioned unobtrusively to sort out the socially undesirable and the potential holdup artist.

Inside they stopped fooling around and hit you

over the head with about four hundred thousand dollars' worth of top-class interior decoration, the cyclamen drapery and forest-green morocco leather school, the Picasso-type murals and the imitation Brancusi sculpture on polished teakwood pedestals. They were so sure of themselves and so determined to preserve the tone of the establishment that there wasn't as much as a single slot machine in the big salon, and conversation stayed down to a murmur even at the crap tables.

But the atmosphere was there, and the pressure stuff, like a charge of high voltage in the air, invisible though you can smell it and hear it clanging in your ears and feel it pricking your skin all the time. No matter where you go—the bookie joint behind a Main Street cigar store, the bingo palace on the boardwalk at Ocean Park, the locker-room poker game at the Uptown Athletic Club—it doesn't make any difference. Some people don't notice it and remain unaffected, they claim; they're the ones who talk about how it's only money and no harm in taking a little flutter once in a while. But the money has nothing to do with it. The money is just a convenient symbol, a tallying device. It's the pressure that counts, like the kick of a heroin shot, and this involves nothing as simple as sweating out the risk of going broke or the chance of getting rich bucking the odds. The house knows, of course, and will maintain correctly that it is in the business of selling entertainment. It merely happens that for some of us this particular form of entertainment works out in a somewhat debilitating manner.

They had three roulette setups going full blast
when I came in, and a fourth just opening up to
take care of the overflow crowd around the
others. I had to stop my hands from hurting me
making fists, and my feet from making a spec-
tacle out of me running. That made me miss the
last available seat—a woman in a wispy cloud of
voile and gold sequins who looked surprisingly
like the young Elizabeth Taylor slammed a volup-
tuous white shoulder into my shirtfront and
grabbed the chair away from me with all the accomplished finesse of a veteran linebacker.

The croupier favored us with a glance that was
mildly disapproving. He was a small, grizzled old
man with a bristling gray toothbrush mustache
and a mottled, liver-spotted complexion, who
held himself ramrod-erect in his shabby tuxedo
of a very old-fashioned cut, like a long-retired
French colonial officer. He accepted two of my
five remaining hundred-dollar bills without quite
shrugging them off, peered at them briefly to
check for slush marks, and slowly pushed across
a stack of ten octagonal magenta chips. To pick
them up I had to jostle the woman in sequins,
who was spreading herself all over the board,
scattering her own chips on a dozen numbers.
The wheel was already spinning, the ball whispering dryly in the groove.

I forced myself to relax. The only way to play
roulette is on a hunch, a lucky inspiration; the
game is the exact opposite of betting on the
races, where you've got to depend on form and
advance information. To my surprise, I didn't
feel any hunches, or anything much at all, except

a vague sort of notion that the red was coming up and due for a run. I almost had to talk myself into testing it out with a single chip, and then when I dropped it on the board the ball was already clicking home and the old croupier disdainfully snapped back my bet with a flick of the rake. *"Rien ne va plus, m'sieu."*

"Sorry...."

The number was thirty, red. The woman who looked like Elizabeth Taylor was on it, *à cheval*, but she'd lost more on other bets than she could cash in on that one. I had to jostle her again to pick up my lone rejected chip, and she glanced up at me with a scowl of irritation. Already the ball was racing down the groove again; the house did not believe in wasting time. Palm Springs has only from Christmas to Easter to shake you down.

The shape of the red on the board suddenly reminded me of that king of diamonds I had enclosed with Lorna's scarf. But in cards the king's number is thirteen, obviously unlucky, and black on the roulette layout. Still, it was a hunch, if it did amount to betting on myself by symbol. I reached over and dropped two chips on thirteen, which happened to be vacant. I meant to make it five, but something checked me. Then, at the last instant, with the ball already whirring down the slope of the wheel and skittering off the chromium ridges, I hurriedly reached once more and pushed the bet over on red twelve, the queen's number, and vacant also. It was a silly thing to do, and I've never gone back on myself like that before, but it got done somehow. It didn't even strike me as anything very odd, or make me feel especially excited.

The little ball bounced back off the wheel, skirled around in another complete circuit, bounced again and dropped quietly to rest. The croupier's rake pointed nonchalantly, swept the board and returned briskly, pushing a stack of fourteen square blue chips toward the center. The woman with the predatory white shoulders started to pull them in.

"Excuse me, please," I said, carefully polite. "My bet, I believe."

The look she gave me came straight out of the deep-freeze locker.

"Were you speaking to me?"

"Yes, ma'am. With your permission. Those are my chips you're picking up."

"They are not." She did not even sound particularly indignant about it; her tone was more contemptuous than anything. "And if you don't mind, I wish you'd kindly move away from here. I can't bear people leaning over me."

The croupier, two fingers poised over the wheel, regarded us with a coldly venomous displeasure. "One moment, *m'sieu, 'dame*," he murmured, holding up his free hand just above the shoulder as if in admonishment.

"One moment yourself," I said. "What's the big idea? You should know who won if she doesn't."

He stared right through me stolidly, as if I were not there at all. Of the crowd around the table no one had even bothered listening to us. The board was already covered with bets on the next spin.

He glanced at it in quick appraisal and released the ball. An arm in a white mess-jacket sleeve sliced under my elbow and pulled me around.

"Well, how about that," said a crisply cheerful voice in. my ear. "The pride of Hollywood and Vine. Bailey. Well, gee whiz!"

If I hadn't known better, I might have thought he was actually glad to see me. He was a full head taller than my own six feet, and as lean as a whip, with a darkly tanned, darkly saturnine professional hoodlum's mug creased into a smile of greeting that looked almost genuine. His manner of guiding me away from the table and out of the room onto the patio gave every appearance of the courteously sociable, but his grip on my arm was one I couldn't have broken without a roughhouse on the spot.

"Nice going, Max," I said bitterly. "They need your talents, if that's how they're operating here."

"Aw, now, Bailey, relax. Don't you know better 'n to argue with the ladies?" He was beaming on me now as he released my elbow, clapping me on the back like an older brother dispensing the punch line of a dirty limerick. He winked at me and palmed two twenty-dollar chips with a flourish, slipped them into my breast pocket and playfully knuckled my chin. "All square now, see?" he chortled. "No hard feelings, huh, Bailey? How come you down here? You slumming or something?"

"If I told you," I said, "you wouldn't believe me, Max."

His smirk widened to the point of obscenity.

"Aw, now, you know me, Bailey. I'm just a pushover for class. Remember me to the boys at Louie's, will ya?" He started to stroll away and winked again over his shoulder. "Don't change your bets, and don't mess with the ladies, please, sir," he aimed at me as a parting shot.

I hung on the bar for a while, nursing a Tom Collins instead of my grievance. I'd been around the mulberry bush too often and too long to be put off by the incident, and for some obscure reason the money did not seem to matter very much. I wasn't even in any great hurry to return to the game room, whereas normally nothing could have stopped me from plunging right back in.

Two hard-faced young blondes in almost identical black satin dinner pajamas came striding in and planted their feet on the brass rail beside me. They ordered bourbon, straight; their bearing was rather like that of a couple of otherwise conscientious workmen taking a break in the middle of a heavy afternoon. "That wop!" one of them protested with a funny mixture of disparagement and awe.

The other one intently consulted her mirror in the execution of a major and much needed repair job. Her open purse on the bar was bulging with chips. "What do you care, hon?" she demanded soberly. "He's dishing it out, isn't he? What do you want, blood?"

"No, but *she* does," said the first one balefully.

"The old bag who's with him, you mean? I think it's just an act. The little shrimp on her shirttail, somebody told me he's her husband. They came all together in the same party."

"Nuts. She's trying to skin him alive, and he loves it. . . ."

The second blonde abandoned the powder puff long enough to toss her Perrier down the hatch in one quick, practiced motion. "Jealous, hon?" she inquired sweetly.

"Jealous, schmealous! A million two they pay for him singing a couple of lousy songs in a picture. And they say with him all you need is a good fast line that winds up ah-ah, mustn't touch. . . ."

I coughed discreetly, but they were both too preoccupied with their troubles to realize that this was not the little girls' room. "Give him time," said the one with the mirror, "he's having so much fun. What gets me is the little guy making like he don't know the score. *Now, angel face.* . . ." she mimicked nastily, sniffing in disgust.

Her companion giggled without amusement. I slipped off my stool and wandered back into the main salon. Rita Jones was holding court at the big chemin-de-fer table, off to the left in the double-window bay. She wore the white peek-aboo dress, and she was pouring on the charm like a musical-comedy actress on premiere night with a tough audience to satisfy. On one side Burt was making himself small in her shadow, slumping way down in his chair, looking sulky and resentful. On the other sat a squat, solid, middle-aged citizen in cream-colored slacks and a scarlet lumberman's shirt open at the neck. He

was very dark, with a plump, oval, olive-
complexioned physiognomy, gleaming, romantic
hazel eyes and a tooth-flashing smile. It was a
face that should have been easy enough to recognize, except for the fact that it was normally
displayed to its public with the mouth open wide
and dispensing a reasonably effective brand of
operatic aria.

My first impulse was to get out of there but
fast. I wanted no part of Mr. Alfredo Vanni,
famous Metropolitan Opera baritone and motion
picture star. Then halfway to the door I thought
better of it. Maybe it was plain curiosity that
made me turn back, or some fool idea about finding out exactly what I was up against. The excuse
I trumped up for myself was that I wanted to
make sure Lorna Ryan wasn't there, although I
knew she wouldn't be.

The chemmy table was even more crowded
with spectators than the other facilities of the
house, and the game appeared to have plenty of
zip. There were a lot of those coarse blue
hundred-dollar markers and quite a few white
and gold thousand-dollar plaques scattered
about, and many patrons did not even bother
with them, casually tossing in the long green
straight from the hip. The banker's shoe was
really traveling; no one seemed able to hang on
to it for more than a couple of coups, and no one
seemed willing, for that matter. After watching a
few minutes I soon realized that what everybody
wanted was to get it back into Vanni's hands as
quickly as possible. He was the only one who'd
put up real money, and it was decidedly comical,

the tacit conspiracy they had among themselves
not to call banco on him. Instead there would be
a scramble to cover him, more or less equitably,
the way buzzards have to live with each other,
and just as promptly the cards would roll over
and bite off his arm. He'd get back some of his
losses in peanuts while the shoe steamed around
another fast circuit, but the instant it pulled up
before him, bang!

He didn't seem to mind a bit, or to be at all
aware of how they were ganging up on him. He
would throw back his head and laugh from the
belly like the bass drum every time he got stung,
and roll his fat black cigar from one corner of his
loose-lipped, cavernous singer's mouth to the
other. He would openly hold hands with Rita
Jones, playing up to her studiedly sinuous co-
quetries, and not quite so openly neck with her
when he judged they were for the moment out of
the focus of general observation. Then he would
briefly pretend to ignore her altogether and con-
centrate on the game with a mock-ferocious
scowl, or plunge into a long-winded anecdote,
complete with expressively histrionic gestures,
while the houseman made up the shoe again and
collected the table fees. The whole performance
was by no means one that made him look silly, or
particularly gullible. It all came perfectly
naturally to him. He was very much accustomed
to being the center of attraction like that, accustomed to sounding off and enjoying his own
popularity, and picking up the check for same.

"Five t'ousan' dollar!"

He didn't have all that much of an accent, but

he had fun laying it on, low-comedy fashion, the dressing-room scene in *Pagliacci*. There was the usual scuffle and flurry to cover. I barely managed to get the two chips on the line that Max had so thoughtfully refunded me. Burt Jones was high man for a grand. He reached for the cards reluctantly, as if they were likely to burn his fingers. He peeked under the corners, frowned bleakly and turned up six-deuce of spades.

Mr. Alfredo Vanni released a hearty chuckle, waved his cigar in a royal command for silence and gave us the old stage business of studying his hand, rolling his eye and showing us his first card, a queen of clubs. The second might still have been an eight, or even a nine, but I knew from his manner that the pattern was simply repeating itself, and several players were already grinning acquisitively in anticipation.

"Baccarat," announced the houseman, formally and without interest. The little wooden rake captured the bank and sent chips flying in all directions of the compass. The tall young Navy lieutenant next to Burt Jones cashed his hundred, mopped his brow with a sweat-soaked handkerchief, rose uncertainly and wandered off in obvious search of liquid refreshment. I slipped into his seat—quickly enough, this time, to beat the competition by inches—and picked up my own modest profits.

The second card had been a queen of diamonds.

The shoe started traveling again, and we had us another round of taking in each other's washing. Not a single bank ran over a thousand dollars.

Rita Jones had recognized me, and she blinked at me occasionally like a cat who'd seen me put the cream away in the icebox. Burt chose to ignore me altogether, contenting himself with running a nervous hand through his skimpy gray hair and glumly watching the game. I was winning steadily, without getting much of a boot out of it. By the time the shoe arrived in front of me I had something just under six hundred in chips stacked up.

Somebody said, "Shoot the works," in a bored tone of voice, and pushed out the stack rather clumsily so that a couple of chips fell off the top. It took me a second or two to realize that the voice and the nonchalance were my own. I was looking at a dozen pairs of scornfully lifted eyebrows here and there, and listening to a sudden raise in the mumble of general conversation. It took them a little while to cover me— I'd caught most of them more or less off guard. A matronly brunette in a classic black chiffon that put most of her capacious, angrily tanned bosom on display across the table had been the first to grasp opportunity by the forelock, and was into me for three centuries. I dealt myself deuce-three and watched her hesitate almost imperceptibly before she dropped the marker on her cards.

I smiled at her fondly and slipped an ace of spades from the shoe, as if all it took was a matter of pushing the right button. The mumbling stopped abruptly; the little rake swooped down and exposed her king-five and went to work for me. "Bets, please," intoned the houseman, not quite shrugging his shoulders.

The rush was already on. The big Italian in the scarlet shirt took a sudden interest and got on the line with five coarse blue chips. It was the first time he had noticed me at all, and the smirk he bestowed upon me was strictly from Figaro good-naturedly kidding the village squire. I didn't like that, for no very good reason, and hurriedly inspected my hand, and showed him a natural—the nine of hearts, with the jack to give it body.

He threw up his arms and laughed his formidable belly laugh. There were a few polite titters joining in, but the crowd was watching me narrowly now, waiting to see the color of my skin. I had twenty-three hundred and sixty dollars' worth of chips and bills before me, and they expected me to retire. I wanted very much to drag about half, but the rules don't allow it; in chemmy you put up or shut up. Burt Jones shot a glance in my direction that could have meant anything: curiosity, warning, pity, contempt.

"Let it ride," I said loudly, surprised that the sting wasn't there, or the chill between my kidneys.

"Banco," said Mr. Alfredo Vanni, promptly and with considerable emphasis as if this was exactly what he had been waiting for.

The crowd delivered a collective hissing noise of disappointment; it had almost forgotten the word, and it wanted its share of the kill. The big Italian pushed out some chips, produced an old-fashioned black morocco pin-seal wallet and peeled off a crisp new bill. He made quite a production out of kissing it goodbye, dropping it on the stack, smiling at me and caressing Rita

Jones's plump white arm all the way up to her neck.

I felt myself taking stock and trying to subdue the dizziness behind my eyes. This was not really money, but it was a lot more than I'd had a shot at for a long, long time, and the tantalizing part of it was that it would amount to just about enough of a stake to spring me. With five G's in my jeans I could be over the hills before morning, buy into a filling station in Kokomo, Indiana, and stay out of trouble for a spell. *Oh, golly! Just what the psychiatrist ordered!* The Ryan girl's cool, childish little voice rang clearly in my ears.

"Banco is made," said the houseman with a trace of irritation.

I glared at him and slid cards from the shoe across the table's slick green baize. My jovial opponent examined his hand and winced elaborately, as if the naked blade of a dagger had been shown to him. I was looking at a six myself, blankly, and waiting for him to make up his mind.

He flashed me another big mouthful of brilliant white teeth. "Ah, Santa Maria, you 'ave me over zee barrel, *signore!*"

"You want a card?"

"*Si, si,* I do. If you please."

The seven of clubs—it was still pretty much a fifty-fifty proposition, because the rules allow the bank to draw to six or seven, and the odds against improving a six are themselves around three to one. I hesitated, squeezed a sickly grin into my lips and pushed back the shoe.

I knew he had two queens again before he got

around to turning them over. This time, of course, they were working for him. For a moment the table seemed to rock under my elbows, and the crowd's instant relapse from dead silence into a buzz of conversation sounded like distant waves breaking on the beach. I was up on my feet before the little rake had finished removing the pile of chips before me. Nobody paid any attention, except for a half-dozen spectators without seats, who were converging on mine in a hurry. Mr. Alfredo Vanni had immediately lost interest and was once more concentrating on the lady in the white lamé dress. Burt Jones had the shoe and carelessly tossed in his three-hundred-dollar minimum.

The two hard-faced blondes had left the bar when I drifted back there with the tide. The Filipino who had served me before took one look at me and came up with a double Johnnie Walker. He did not leave the bottle, but he kept it handy. My wristwatch said 10:35.

A full two hours later I was still sitting there. Not drunk, not sober, not anything in particular. My normal reaction to a lot of Scotch is to doze off, but in this case I wasn't the least bit sleepy, and the faculty that might be facetiously referred to as my mind had remained very clear indeed—much too clear for comfort. The woman who looked like Elizabeth Taylor had made an entrance, ordered a whiskey sour, recognized me and flounced out again without paying the check. Max Gonzalez, the bouncer who liked class, had lounged by a couple of times, winking at me, happy to see me relax. New faces and several old, familiar ones had come floating in and out of my limited range of vision. By one o'clock the Filipino had grown a little slow on the trigger.

"You are tired, maybe, *señor*? I get someone to drive you home, hah?"

"Get someone to pour two jiggers of Scotch into my glass," I told him coldly.

He nodded and made the customary bland face for me and wandered back to the cash register. I saw him reach for the wrong no-sale key, the one that would only bring Max in again to get whimsical with me. I got up and strolled out through the big salon, unhurriedly but without looking anywhere except straight ahead.

Outside the sharp desert night air cut through my smoke-filled lungs like a knife. The scent of the climbing roses on the fencework along the walk to the parking-lot gate reminded me of a broken perfume bottle. There was plenty of moon, chalk white and sneering frostily, lording it over an ashen sky. Somehow I got rolling, out of the lot and down the driveway and on the road, without so much as scraping gears or being struck by a bolt of lightning.

The Duesenberg caught up with me just short of the Onowanda Park intersection. It had headlights as bright as airport beacons and a horn that blared the first five notes of "O Sole Mio," but loud and strictly on pitch. It had a special, custom-built, open phaeton body that glistened as black as a praying mantis, and a great big brute of an engine that whispered like a wheat field in the breeze, and a black chauffeur in a powder-blue cossack dolman with silver piping. It pulled past and away from me like a sigh of disgust, slowed perfunctorily for the stop sign at the crossroads and bore left toward town going ninety in no special hurry.

I started to turn right for home, then changed my mind on a sudden crazy impulse and wrestled the wheel around again. The Ford obediently rattled along in pursuit of the black convertible, which was already little more than a distant pinprick of lights along the highway. For thirty seconds or so those lights continued to recede before their beams shifted abruptly, slashed off the pavement at an angle, disappeared briefly behind a greasewood copse, and twisted half circle into the grounds of a sizable Monterey villa on the edge of town.

The Ford coasted limply past the mouth of the driveway while I snarled at myself for making like a square from Delaware. There was nothing in this for me—I was just wasting time, effort and gasoline, tagging along after a guy who owed me nothing and who had a perfect right to rent himself a Palm Springs mansion while his favorite girl friend was staying at a nearby hotel on what she fondly imagined to be a professional engagement. *I'm expecting a telephone call after dinner. A business call. . . .*

I shrugged and tooled the car around and hightailed it back to the Hacienda del Sol, a comfortable ten-minute drive. When I pulled into the courtyard a small yellow Buick coupe with California plates cut in ahead of me on two wheels and careered drunkenly into its parking slot, bumping the wall. The Joneses climbed out of it and wandered off into the compound, not touching each other.

They were gone before I entered the park, but a light snapped on in their bungalow when I passed it, and there was a clatter of venetian blinds being adjusted, immediately followed by the muffled wrangling of their voices.

It did not occur to me to be intelligently interested in the conversation. It was partly the Scotch and partly the ordinary curiosity of human nature that made me stop on the lawn under the window and bend an ear. Not much of it came through the blinds, or made any sense. There was none of that "angel face" stuff, but in snatches it didn't at first sound like more than a routine bedtime argument.

". . . overplayed your hand again. . . ."

". . . think you're so smart. It worked out all right, didn't it?"

". . . his way of giving us the brush-off. Can't tell until tomorrow. The way you handled it, we may have trouble keeping him in line."

"Oh, don't be silly. You've got to play up to these wops to get anywhere."

". . . don't like the looks of it. This character big-eyeing the Ryan doll. . . ."

". . . that meathead? He seems harmless enough to me."

". . . following us around? You remember what Doc said. If they catch us muscling in. . . ."

"They don't know us, honey."

"Yeah, yeah. Here, gimme a hand with this, will ya, please?"

He was coming too near the window to suit me.
I crept away from there behind a yard of frown
and quietly crossed the greensward. The moon
was still sneering at me, and the chorus of
crickets sounding off in a steady and dryly sardonic refrain. From my own front porch I saw no
lights anywhere except in the adjoining bungalow. The bedroom blinds were up and there was
movement behind the screen. I stared at it hard,
blinking when darkness closed in suddenly with
an audible click of the switch, and then I realized
that the girl in white lace pajamas had been
Lorna Ryan, retiring for the night.

morning. You look as (today you can't reason

I snapped a trin th... probably no wore
that fashion, and non...
the rush... while w... was some room
left. 30... nun is p...ith boxes, scratch
oats, a cradle boar... the lid and on a
rub-ober chunt ai...number, and two pie
table...und as the t... the book are a been
THE ... ISLAND 95

9

ON THURSDAY MORNING not even the mockingbird in the olive tree outside my window
could wake me up in time for breakfast. The
blinds in the bungalow next door had been
drawn against the sun, and the air-conditioning
intake gadget on the roof was humming. The guy
from room service came whistling behind his cad-
dy across the lawn and brought me two aspirins,
an omelet and a pot of black coffee. That gave
me just about the strength to change into my
shorts and stagger on out to the pool.

Mrs. Eve Garand reclined on a steamer chair
under the third umbrella from the left, the one
with the red and white polka dots. She wore
baggy old corduroy slacks and the halter from a
two-piece bathing suit decorated in a somewhat
faded green fig-leaf design. Oddly enough this
kind of sartorial anarchy became her pretty well
and served somehow to temper the hard lines of
her toast-brown body, the almost masculine arrogance of her lean, hawk-nosed features. But
her hand wave was as much of a royal command
as any gesture currently on tap in the western
hemisphere.

''Sit down, my friend. I shan't wish you good

morning. You look as though you might resent
it.''

I managed a grin that was probably no worse
than fatuous, and hooked a leg over one side of
the garden table where there was some room
left: she had it piled high with books, scratch
pads, a Corona portable with the lid still on, a
half-empty mint julep tumbler and two big
ashtrays filled to the brim. The book she'd been
reading lay ajar on her flat sunburned stomach. It
was Humphrey Slater's *Conspirator*, of all
things.

''They tell me you're a writer,'' I said. It sounded as bright as a moron on a quiz show.

''Don't call the cops.'' She shook out her heavy
gray bangs solemnly. ''I'm out on probation.
Anyway, you're not the injured party. My stuff's
for women, about women.''

''I wasn't complaining. It sounds like a pretty
good deal.''

''It's hell,'' she told me briskly. ''I'm always
begging them to take me back on the chain gang,
but they want me to suffer. How about you? A
musician's life should be rather satisfying, in
many ways. They usually seem to me so wrapped
up in their art that nothing else has much of a
chance to worry them. But on the other hand
they must do so much traveling they can never
settle down and strike roots.''

I said I supposed that covered a lot of people
and a lot of territory these days, and she smiled
her benevolent smile for me. It had a slightly
feline cast to it.

''Don't be so damned noncommittal with me,

young man. People are my business. I like them, and I'm fixing to like you if you'll give me half a chance. Tell me about yourself—get it off your chest instead of all this caginess and moping around."

I laughed, not very heartily. "Not much to tell...."

"Oh, go on with you. Of course there is, and a lot more than I've any business hearing about, I daresay."

It would have been a pleasure to go debonair on her and bow myself out of there with a few well-chosen suavities. The only trouble was that for all I knew she might be holding the stakes besides publishing the dope sheet and handicapping the horses.

"This is most flattering," I said, and firmly suppressed a shudder. "I hope you realize that I'm like everybody else. My favorite subject is me, and I love to talk about it. Where shall we start?"

"Just go ahead and talk." She lighted a fresh cigarette from the stub of the old one before I had a chance of coming up with a match. She was using one of those long black holders that have a cartridge of chemicals in them to filter out most of the kick. "Start anywhere you like, my friend. I promise none of it will be used against you."

The sun was bearing down on the back of my neck. I mopped up the sweat with a towel and said casually enough, "It still isn't much of a story, any way you look at it. I was born in '45— White Plains, New York. One of those wartime deals: mother was very young and beautiful, dad wore cavalry boots with spurs that jingled. She was impressed, but the Nazis weren't. . . ."

"Go on," she said placidly, watching me from behind the glint in her sunglasses. "You're doing all right now."

"Yes, ma'am. So that left her with me, and the insurance. We had it pretty good, though. The family helped out at first, and by the time I was six or seven she'd already made a name for herself on the concert stage."

Mrs. Garand nodded thoughtfully. "Lillian Bailey," she said. "Of course."

"You knew her?" I demanded, more startled than incredulous.

"I remember an interview with her in Chicago, when I was a sob sister on the *Tribune* back in the fifties. She played the harp like an angel, and she was a hell of a nice gal, but your father's name wasn't Bailey, young man."

"Do we have to go into that?"

"We don't. But you should, for yourself, and get it out of your system. Bastards have been respectable for a long time."

"I'm not complaining," I assured her. My headache was killing me, but it doesn't make sense to start something you can't finish. "There's no question about it, mother was tops. But you asked me to talk about myself. I wasn't any prodigy, but I managed to major in music at Columbia. Not good, not bad. She wanted to send me to Europe, the Paris conservatory, enjoy the advantages she'd missed herself. Only I knew I didn't have the stuff in me. I got a job with Buddy Van Zell at the Bamboo Room in Pittsburgh. It was the year after that, when she'd come down to visit me, a speeding ambulance hit the sidewalk right in front of the hotel and smashed her to bits.''

Mrs. Garand said evenly, ''That was a long time ago.'' The glint in her sunglasses did not waver.

''That's right,'' I said. ''Twelve years ago my last birthday. So I was twenty-two, and she'd taught me to swim by myself. There was some money coming to me, too, and I found a booker who was willing to take a chance. Two months later I opened at the Coronet Lodge in Colorado Springs, with a brand-new crew. Not good, not bad.''

''You're making that sound like a motto for yourself.''

''Sorry. It just slipped out. We made out okay, as hotel bands go, until the draft broke up the game. You don't want to hear about the Rover Boys on kitchen police, or Bailey goes to war, do you?''

''I'm listening.''

''For a writer,'' I said, ''you pick the darnedest verbs, ma'am. Anyway, there wasn't much to that, either. I got to be assistant boss of a small fire base in Binh Duong Province that somehow irritated the V.C. a lot. They tried us a dozen times in four, five months and lost a bunch of people. After a while some of us got to go home and some didn't. I had no special place to go, so I went to California, for the climate, only on my first day in a sports shirt the cops hauled me out of an orange-juice stand on Hollywood Boulevard for busting up the joint. They told me later I'd

been irked with the proprietor—he wouldn't
listen when I ordered him to open fire, there
were some V.C. sappers coming down the block.
Don't worry, they talked me out of these incon-
vénient notions at the veterans' hospital. They
were awfully patient about it. And what's *your*
hobby, ma'am, when you're not writing books or
liking people?"

"I play croquet," she told me calmly. "You
must try it sometime. There aren't any kings
with holes behind them, and it's a very popular
game in Bermuda."

The jolt went clean through me before I recognized the source of her information. "Oh, sure,
Bermuda," I said inanely, steadying myself with
an effort. "Yes, ma'am. No holes behind the
kings in that deal. I see where Miss Ryan has been
doing a little talking to you, too."

"My dear boy, you're old enough to know that
all women are born gossips."

We looked at each other for a while in silence.
She reached for her mint julep and drained it like
a man; the movement dislodged Slater's *Conspirator* from her stomach. I slid off the table
and retrieved the book for her and remained
standing there, without quite allowing my foot to
trace a circle on the tiles.

"I bet you like her," I said at last, forcing a grin
and feeling like the village idiot.

"Certainly I do. Lorna's a very sweet child,
although I should imagine that most men are
scared to death of her. They've all become so accustomed to sophistication in a pretty girl that
the lack of it sends them up a tree much faster

than a scalded cat. She was raised in convent school back East, you know. Now that I come to think of it, both of you are orphans."

It seemed to me as if she hesitated almost imperceptibly on that last word, and I had trouble hanging on to my grin. "She scares me all right," I said. "You must've heard me throw that bobble yesterday on the piano."

"I heard you, yes." Mrs. Garand allowed her sunglasses to slip half an inch below the bridge of her thin, hawklike nose and inspected me briefly across the rims. There was nothing trivial about the inspection; once again she reminded me of a scientist examining a somewhat doubtful specimen. "The question is," she observed rather dryly, "how much difference it would make to either of you."

"Now there's a point," I said, dropping the grin in a hurry. "But you should know that at this stage a man is usually too muddled to take sensible stock of the situation. Besides, there seems to be very little time, and worst of all, I get the impression that the line forms to the right."

"Oh, Lorna has this young whippersnapper on a string who considers himself engaged to her, and who drove her down in his fancy courtin' flivver," she informed me calmly. "He's the Bel Air society type, too much money and too much swash; she'll know better than to get stuck with him. I suppose there's quite a wolf pack snapping at her pretty ankles back in town, but so far none of them have shown up here. You're a funny guy, Bailey, and I do mean peculiar. I daresay it's high time you got wise to yourself and stopped floundering around in a swamp of silly complexes and guilty feelings. I still don't believe you're much bothered about this girl, but if you are, a little competition is hardly likely to do more than make you use your elbows. Which might be an excellent idea at that.'' She swung her legs off the chair and rose lazily, stretching herself with the unabashed indolence of a woman who has long ceased to care about appearance. ''Lobster Newburg for lunch,'' she reminded me. ''But you wouldn't be hungry, I know. Class dismissed.''

I watched her disappear in a long, swinging stride among the tangerine trees and the date palms. The pool lay deserted again, shimmering quietly, its blue of an almost malevolent intensity. The moment she was gone I flopped on the nearest rubber mattress and lay sweating and shaking and breathing fast for what seemed like a very long time, as if after an excess of heavy physical exercise.

When deliberate reason finally came back on top, things began to look up a little. I decided I'd held up my end, after all, and that Eve Garand was nothing but a nosy old witch with a knack for upsetting people and worrying confidences out of them by sheer force of insinuation. The old sob-sister technique—she could even afford to come right out and admit as much. It amused me to consider that actually she might prove herself helpful yet. She undoubtedly had matchmaking ideas. Not the simple ones of a frustrated spinster, but the kind a chemist has in mind when he's fingering his test tubes.

The shakes left me at last. I went back to the

bungalow, showered and shaved carefully, brushed my hair until it looked right, worked on myself the way a handler grooms a show dog. I phoned the gift shop and had them send over a ten-dollar box of candy, charged to my account. When the bellhop came whistling across the lawn with it and knocked on Lorna's door, I was right behind him.

She was wearing something cool and simple in green-checkered cotton, the least bit tousled from lying down in it most of the day, and she blinked at the box. "A sudden inspiration," I said. "It came to me just like that. She looks so frail and delicate, I told myself, it must be because nobody ever sends her a box of candy."

The bellhop smirked and got out from under my feet. The girl in the green wrap stared at me in wide-eyed astonishment.

"But you shouldn't have. Really."

"I couldn't think of any other way to make you go swimming with me."

She frowned doubtfully. "I was reading a book," she told me. "One of Eve's. If I get out in the sun too much, Mr. Biedermayer will be mad. He says he has to use too many filters on me."

"He the fellow who's supposed to take your picture here? The one who was to phone last night?"

"Yes, of course. But some rush jobs came in and he said he'd be delayed in town for a few days."

"I bet he told you to enjoy yourself while you were waiting."

"How did you. . . .? Oh, all right. You'd better

come in and sit down while I change.'' She was suddenly gay, as if we were plotting to steal a march on the indulgent Mr. Biedermayer. Her nails slit deftly through the gaudy cellophane wrapper of the candy box. ''Aren't they super! You'll have some, won't you? When a man gives me candy it's usually just an excuse for indulging his own sweet tooth.'' She smiled at me bewitchingly and slipped into the bedroom munching.

I let out my breath and sat on the arm of a chair. Her living room was a duplicate of mine: same size and shape, same phony French provincial pieces, same carpet, same chintzes. The only difference was a matter of atmosphere. Not the copy of *Harper's Bazaar* on the table, or the green leather handbag and matching gloves flung carelessly on the couch, or the faint trace of Shalimar in the air—these were no more than props, and commonplace enough, lacking significance. What affected me may easily have been simple imagination, or the backlash of conscience still too little flexible for the demands made upon it. The room was, after all, only one of scores built and furnished exactly alike: modern, not very large, and impersonally cheerful. There was no reason why it should have given me a sense of danger, of alarm and high excitement. Not then, on Thursday afternoon at three o'clock.

Lorna Ryan emerged from the bedroom in one of those beach-coat arrangements, a crimson print piqué in three or four instalments, the style that is designed to let the ladies do a genteel sort of striptease for you at the poolside. She executed a languid pirouette to show it off. "You like?"

"I'll buy it." Joe Cornero's gruffly scornful voice rang in my ears. *They're worse than actresses, Mr. Bailey, and that's for sure. All they ever care about is what they can see in the mirror....*

She slipped a small, cool hand under my arm and laughed at me. It was a friendly laugh that wiped out every one of the exotic-orchid contours in her face and made her suddenly appear like any other bright young thing with a new outfit for the beach. "You couldn't *buy* it," she assured me, half-seriously. "Josette designed it specially for me. And you didn't take a piece of my candy!"

"I'll have one now," I said, and quickly, lightly, kissed her small, upturned, strawberry-luscious mouth.

She did not draw back or remove her hand, but she stiffened and pulled me along to the door. "I didn't mean that," she told me, not too steadily.

Outside the jitters vanished as promptly as they'd come upon me in that living room. Our walk through the park, arm in arm, drew an assortment of disapproving stares from the occupants of front-porch lounges as we passed on our way. Two wrinkled old Japanese gardeners spraying date palms in the orchard paused long enough to sneer at us and nudge each other. The pool with its accessories was all ours, the Garand woman, her books and her typewriter nowhere in evidence; only the brimming ashtrays and the empty julep tumbler were still there. The water was warm, almost enervating. The scent of the tangerine trees hung sweet and heavy in the parched, hot desert air.

A private swimming pool, under such circumstances, makes a fine, serviceable setting for a fast job of fraternizing with the enemy. It strongly suggests, after all, the physical intimacy of sharing a bathtub, and stops short only at mere details, such as a few scraps of cloth or the application of soap to your partner's back. It takes a girl who is either very clever or very innocent to stand off the scores of possible boarders' tactics in this situation. The fact remains that in two hours of it, with the sun already sharply declining toward the mountains, I did not make a single pass at Lorna Ryan. The simple reason was that she quite obviously did not expect one.

By five-thirty or so she halted a spirited game of toss ball with a gasp of apparently genuine dismay. "Oh, I forgot . . . !"

"What's wrong?"

"You're supposed to take it easy." *You're supposed to get this bim out of my hair.*

"It's all right. I feel swell. You're pretty good medicine for me."

She shook her head decisively and swung herself lithely up the chrome steel ladder to the tile walk. "You mustn't get tired. You'd better rest awhile now, before sundown. Please."

We lay in silence on our backs, on adjoining mattresses, watching the drama of the rapidly lengthening palm tree shadows, and she let me hold her hand, like kids in junior high. The first husky whiffs of the evening breeze came sighing in, still genial enough to dry us quicker than a towel; they were soon due to freshen into squalls that would carry the bite of distant snow. My headache had long disappeared, its place now occupied by a strange mixture of serene contentment and perplexed frustration.

I reminded myself that the deal called for me to make like a wolf, not like a jackass. There was no sense in feeling small about it, or in throwing in my hand. I was doing the lady a favor, whether she knew it or not—it wasn't my fault that she'd got herself involved with the Hitchcock dynasty in such a tactless manner. She'd be better off now if she let me take her in tow as per schedule. A trip to Bermuda wouldn't be so bad. Not as bad as whatever they'd cooked up for her in case Bailey couldn't slip her the business.

She squeezed my hand just then. "I'm getting chilly."

"Think we should turn in?"

"I guess so. It's nice out here, isn't it?"

"Uh-huh."

"Will you play the piano for me?"

I jerked my head around. She was looking at me without a trace of mockery or self-consciousness, solemnly expectant. She had removed her cap, and the breeze was ruffling through her glossy black locks affectionately as if it enjoyed the privilege.

"Sure, anytime," I said. "But yesterday I didn't do so well, if you remember."

"That was yesterday," she pointed out calmly. "You were worried about something. I could tell."

The bathhouse faces to the southeast and was

already gloomy with the dusk. I slid the patio-
door shut and snapped switches; the small electric log in the fireplace responded in a cheery
glow while on the bar a light sprang up inside the
grinning mountain-lion skull they kept there to
impress you with the frontier flavor of the joint.
This time she sat down next to me behind the
Blüthner—unhesitatingly but with no hint of co-
quetry. This time the jackass in me did not want
to play.

"I'm still worried," I said, and absentmindedly
allowed my hands to ramble on the keyboard.

Any hack pianist can perform in this manner
for hours on end, without thinking, or listening
to himself, or doing anything at all except moving a few muscles long accustomed to expand and
contract by routine coordination, the way a
bicyclist keeps his balance and stays on the road
as a matter of course. What comes out in such
cases is usually a pretty colorless medley of
various popular and semiclassical tunes, the
whistling-butcher-boy kind that sold a million
copies back in '25, the kind that stays put in your
fingers until the day the undertaker straightens
them out on your chest: the early Irving Berlin,
Walter Donaldson, selections from *Rose Marie*
and *Show Boat*, snatches from a Strauss waltz. I
must have done all of those in the next fifteen
minutes, probably quite competently. And all the
time I was looking down into a huge mouthful of
handsome, sparkling, smiling white teeth
clamped firmly on a fat, expensive black cigar.

Banco! Five t'ousan' dollar. . . .

I thought how easy it would be to pin her down

on that one. I could switch to the classics, serve up a piece from *Madama Butterfly* or *La Traviata*, to keep things in character. She'd be a cinch to give the show away and start talking; she'd admitted herself about being a terrible actress. Only there wasn't anything in that for me. It never helps to put them on the spot, making them talk about the other guy. They go coy on you, or remorseful, or just plain annoyed. So he made music, too, and he was a big shot in pictures, and he'd had the inside track with her for a couple of years. That was all right. I was still young, and six feet tall, a hundred and eighty pounds, and I didn't smoke cigars unless somebody made me.

She was watching my hands on the keyboard, the way she'd watched them Tuesday night at the card table, smiling a little, a vague smile of polite disinterest. The queen of diamonds behind the jack, and all the kings were in their counting house. I suppressed a shrug and dragged my attention back to the Blüthner. I was urbanely tinkling away on an old French ballad, one of the first pieces I'd learned as a boy when my mother started to teach me at the age of four—its title was something like "Pleasures of Love," I recalled. It didn't seem to fit the mood exactly. I shifted keys and started improvising to get back into the groove; what was needed here would be more in the nature of a dose of clever schmaltz, I thought. Then one of Jerome Kern's best efforts came to mind, the song we'd featured in a special arrangement with an organ choir effect on our last

tour three years ago, just before things went
haywire.

For sparking purposes, there's no modern com-
poser who can match his stuff in sheer lyrical ardor, both of melody and harmony. Cole Porter is
too sophisticated, Berlin too simple, Youmans too
frivolous, Gershwin too much inclined to com-
promise, too conscious of his own importance. It
is only Kern who will pull all the stops and really
sound like a man going down on his knees:

You are the promised kiss of springtime
That makes the lonely winter seem long
You are the breathless hush of evening
That trembles on the brink of a lovely song. . . .

The words themselves are in the music—no
human voice is needed to convey them. The
Blüthner responded royally, giving me a warm
tenor saxophone effect against a somber bass
counterpoint, fairly dripping with romantic
modulation.

You are the angel glow that lights a star
The dearest things I know are what you are. . . .

A solo clarinet, in the middle register, pleading
from its melancholy heart of seasoned grenadillo
wood and supported by three carefully blended
trombones serenading judiciously in a mellow
legato. It wasn't particularly good, or difficult,
but it was effective, the way a crowbar is effective. It changed the emotional climate in that
room as thoroughly as if Frank Sinatra had made

an entrance fingering his bow tie and looking soulful.

Someday my happy arms will hold you
And someday I'll know that moment divine
When all the things you are, are mine.

The full ensemble, bass sliding down resonantly into the depths of joyful despair, and a single trumpet riding high above the rest, like a handsome young troubadour on a great white stallion. I was actually pleased with it myself and gave it everything I had to offer, winding up in a rapid-fireworks arpeggio, all the way up to high A-flat.

Silence came quivering with the echo of the Blüthner's strings. The girl beside me was not smiling anymore. She stared straight ahead through the window at the pool's reflection of the last few shimmerings of twilight.

"Lorna..." I said. It was the first time I had ever spoken her name.

She turned. The movement brought her face into the shadows, eyes half-closed, lips tarnished suddenly from carmine to a dusky violet. She did not struggle when I pulled her off the bench, and for a few brief seconds my senses registered nothing but darkness, and the elusive fragrance of Shalimar, and the flavor of warm spiced honey. Then my knees started shaking and she pushed me back with unexpected strength, sharply enough to make me stagger.

"You mustn't. Please. I mean it."

"What's wrong?" I demanded stupidly.

"There's nothing wrong. I don't want you to kiss me. Not like this."

"Oh, you know a better way," I said, more bewildered than sarcastic.

She confronted me squarely; she seemed perfectly composed, although I suspected she was very close to tears. "It isn't that," she said naively. "You don't understand. If you were in love with me it would be different, maybe, but you're not. You don't even think you are. Do you?"

My hands were fists, my toes clawing into the rug. "Of course I am," I said thickly.

"No. You're just restless and nervous, after all those bad times in the hospital. And you want to make sure you remember what girls are like—any girl. You're doing this to me only because I happen to be around. It isn't fair, not even to yourself."

"But it's not like that at all!" I protested, sounding about as baffled as a character in a soap opera. "Maybe I've been impatient, but you don't realize—"

"Please don't let's wrangle." She retrieved her arm out of my grasp and administered a sisterly pat to my shoulder. "If you think about it I'm sure you'll agree with me. Impatience doesn't enter into it. When people are in love there's never any doubt, is there?" She was already at the door, although it seemed as if she'd hardly moved, and my legs refused point-blank to help me stop her. "You do play very well," she told me with her parting smile and walked quietly, gracefully away into the gathering darkness of the palm trees.

I sat on the bench for a while with my back to the keyboard, not even swearing at myself. The hard-faced blonde from the Tahquitz Casino bar was scoffing in my ear. *A good fast line that winds up ah-ah, mustn't touch....* Something was wrong all right, some cockeyed little thing had thrown my picture of the situation altogether out of focus. I had no business at all feeling and acting like a college freshman on the morning after his first prom. The pot had been built up too much, and these were table stakes to me.

Of course there wasn't any question that by then I had already fallen for her; if she'd pushed me off the roof of city hall I might have been in better shape. The trouble was, I didn't know about that yet. It's quite a laugh, the way a man will con himself into the firm belief that he has the drop on his emotions. I told myself I'd simply rushed my fences without taking time to scout the course. Maybe I should've listened to the Garand woman's warning. An unsophisticated girl who'd spent most of her life in convent school would need a different approach.

So far I had no other proof that she was Vanni's mistress than that damned detective agency report. But even a detective agency can make mistakes, and I remembered how they'd hedged the real issue. *Subject continues to exercise more than average discretion in behavior.* Mere weasel words they'd used to camouflage their failure to deliver concrete evidence.

It struck me then that I might easily be able to do better. She'd flown out West in March last

year, following Vanni in a matter of weeks after
his return to Hollywood—she'd mentioned it to
me herself and laughed it off, saying she had
been movie-struck. There were at least three
airlines that she might have patronized, but
T.W.A. was the only one that got the movie
trade.

I snapped a finger at myself and made a beeline for the phone extension on the bar. The
clerk in the Hacienda office sounded peeved
with me and made a big show out of getting my
apartment number straight before he'd fur-
nish me a city line. I didn't even care if he
was listening. I wanted information right
away and I knew just exactly where to look for
it.

Bill Jeffers was off duty, but the downtown
reservations desk gave me the number of his
home. I flashed long distance back and got him
on the wire. He was at dinner, judging by the off-
stage clink of crockery, the fretful baby wail,
and Walter Cronkite on TV.

"Who did you say?" It took him something of
an effort to recall the name, and in between he
had to shout for them to close the kitchen door.
"Bailey. . . ? Oh, yeah. Well, gee, Sarge, how are
you? Long time no see. Whaddaya hear from the
gang?"

"All I know is what I read in the newspapers,"
I told him. "Things like you growing up into a big
shot, with a job at T.W.A., a family and everything. Pretty nice work for the lousiest gunner in
Battery C."

"Yes, sir, I'm doing fine," he assured me.

"Well, shucks, it's been ten years, how do you like that! What's with you, Sarge?"

"Nothing much," I said. "You know me, Bill—anything for a gag. Listen, this music store I work for, girl came in today who wants us to deliver a piano on terms. But retail credit doesn't have a rating on her, and the deal looks a little funny. She hasn't been here long and she can't give us any references. So we asked around and got one anyway, only we can't afford to check on it direct. You wanna help us out?"

He was intrigued, just as I knew he would be. "Sure, be glad to, Sarge, but how?"

I told him how. That left him still intrigued, if slightly dubious. He didn't like it, and he didn't think it would do any good. I had to kid him along and coax him into it before he would play ball. Then he wanted to call me back, because he'd have to talk to his own office first, and of course that wouldn't have worked out at all. So I had to improvise a yarn about the switchboard being closed, and promise to call him again in fifteen minutes. He didn't ask me why a music store should need a switchboard.

Those fifteen minutes lasted long enough for me to wear a groove into the rug. The mountain-lion skull kept up its eerily translucent grin. It got so hot in there that I was forced to disconnect the fireplace log and find another towel to mop up the sweat. I almost talked myself into a flat walkout, simply from being tired and hungry and sick of the whole dirty business. But when time was up at last I caught myself pouncing on that phone as if it was fixing to spit in my eye.

Bill Jeffers sounded much impressed, if somewhat scandalized. "Hey, Sarge, this long shot of yours ran in the money. We have the dope on her at records here. I didn't think we would, because New York is where she'd normally have booked. But as it happens our Hollywood office made the reservation and issued a passage voucher. That's the procedure when you're taking care of someone out of town: you mail it to them and they exchange it for a regular ticket at the local office, which has already been advised by teletype."

"That's how I figured it," I said. "You get the name?"

"We wouldn't, not if he'd paid cash. But on the docket there's a note that says paid for by check No. 3228 on the Sherman Oaks branch of the California Security Trust, personal account, Mr. Alfredo Vanni."

"Good deal," I said, riding with the punch. "Thanks very much, Bill. I guess it means we make a sale."

"I guess you do. Say listen, take it easy, will ya, Sarge? That sort of stuff is dynamite if there's a leak."

I forced a chuckle, telling him I knew it was.

On the walk back to my bungalow the desert wind screamed at me like a siren. I had to break into a run again, and wound up on the front porch gasping with my lungs on fire. It brought the Jones woman's admonishment to mind. *Let up on the throttle, handsome, you're burning out a bearing....* Then it occurred to me that I was overlooking something of a bet in failing to keep up with the Joneses. Both of them were evident-

ly pretty well informed, and their bedtime conversation of the night before had seemed to indicate a faintly sinister connection. Moreover,
for some reason Burt had sounded as if he might
actually be afraid of me. The idea struck me as a
little quaint, but I saw no objection to my cashing
in on it if necessary.

Across the lawn, lights blazed through open
shades in both rooms of the Jones domain. I trot-
ted over, still in trunks and robe, and found the
front door half-ajar. Two buxom, trimly uniformed Mexican maids were hustling all over the
place behind vacuum cleaners, dust rags and a
basket of fresh linens. The apartment had
already acquired the bleak, impersonal look of
vacant hotel rooms everywhere.

For no good reason sudden panic squeezed my
stomach into something like a solid rubber ball. I
shouldered past the curiously staring maids and
reached for the house phone on the bedroom
dresser.

"What happened to the party in fifteen?"

The surly clerk in the Hacienda office recognized my voice and contrived to raise an eyebrow
at me in his. "Since that is where you're calling
from, sir, you ought to see for yourself. They
checked out an hour ago."

So Burt's cold feet had run away with him and
made him drop this badger game I had suspected
him of playing on the side. Somehow it seemed to
me even more vitally important now to tackle
both of them, but instantly. Bill Jeffers's tip-off
should have been enough, but after all that trouble I was still dissatisfied. I wanted to make sure I

got the pitch. The notion that I might not really care to think in terms of anything except Miss Lorna Ryan's innocence never quite managed to suggest itself.

The clerk was coughing in my ear impatiently. I bared a fang at him and asked, "You have a forwarding address?"

"No, sir. But if you're interested, it is customary for our guests to sign the register when they arrive."

"That's right," I said. "Get flip with me and give me an excuse to hurry down and bust you in the snoot. It just so happens that I'm working for your boss, fella. What address did they give you on the register?"

He gulped and read it off to me, in such a rush I had to make him tell me twice.

The bungalow next door was dark. She'd be at dinner, and the menu would have brook trout, roast capon and crepes suzette. I dashed into my clothes and sprinted for the parking lot. For me there would be a hamburger at Joe's Drive-in, off Highway 60, east of Riverside.

10

THE INCORPORATED CITY of Formosa, California,
appeared on my motoring map of Los Angeles
county as a tiny speck just off the Harbor Freeway, located strategically within a three-buck
taxi ride from both the dockyards of San Pedro
and the oil refineries of Wilmington. The name
means "beautiful" in Portuguese. I knew that
much, and nothing else, about the place. It didn't
take me long to learn a little more.

They had a banner sign up with a spotlight on it
where the highway entered town. The sign said
Jesus Saves, summarily, as if that were all there
was to it. They must have needed the reminder:
all they had to offer was a mile or two of clapboard frame and ancient yellow brick, dumped
squarely in the middle of an endless stretch of
flat and barren fields. On Main Street the used-
car lots and the shabby real-estate operators
were crowding each other to death; at Main and
First, four corners featured a flyblown little
drugstore, an establishment selling Rabbits on
Ice, the redwood shack of an expert in palmistry,
and a brisk new stucco box labeled Happy Valley
Mortuary. This seemed to be the only intersection with a traffic light, presumably intended to

protect the drunks when they came staggering out of the poolroom next door to the drugstore.

The city hall was something else again, a tall modern sandstone structure set apart from the common herd in a tile-paved square of its own, complete with trees, two hundred feet of lawn, a huge steel flagpole and the only six streetlamps in town. They caught a glitter of chrome and polished brass for me from two big, beautiful, streamlined engines proudly on display behind the open doors of the fire department wing. Across the square a nice, clean, prosperous little glass-brick edifice proclaimed itself the home of the Formosa *Enquirer*.

I kept on going at the legal rate of twenty-five past all this impressive array of civic progress. The sixteen-hundred block on South Main turned out to be at the very edge of open country. It was occupied on the east side by a couple of Quonset huts casually deposited on the verge of a stretch of dark pastureland and casually marked Formosa Airport. On the west side rose a large, solid-looking, windowless, white concrete-block building, brilliantly floodlighted and sporting a roof sign in flashing red and green neon that announced Club Gaucho. Behind it, less than half a mile away, the ocean muttered sullenly against the cliffs.

The night was still a pup, but business seemed to be pretty good: the big cement parking lot was jammed to capacity, and cars were stacked along the shoulders of the road for several hundred yards. Most of them needed a wash job and a turn in the body-repair shop. I rolled the Ford to the end of the line and wandered back. The brightly trimmed canvas marquee split like a Y toward separate entrances. Five aces spread into a neon fan were featured over the revolving door to starboard, while the one to port displayed the female form divine arising from a cocktail glass.

An elderly police sergeant in full-dress blues assisted me from the foyer, in pushing through the door below the poker hand. His ruddy moon face smiled attentively, listening to me. "Jones, did you say, sir? There's a good many customers here by that name."

"This one's no customer."

He shook his fat gray head and scratched behind one ear. "See Mr. Norman," he advised. "Him that's the pit boss in there. He'll know what it's all about."

In there was quite a situation. The air- conditioned room ran half the building's size under a dome-shaped ceiling painted apple green, from which at least two dozen banks of fluorescent lights bathed everything in a hard, impersonal green glare. Something like sixty poker tables ran wide open, with a waiting line of eager candidates for seats straining against the velvet rope. Surprisingly the place would have seemed very quiet indeed except for the dry ruffle of the chips like locust wings in flight.

A spare, benign old gentleman neatly attired in double-breasted serge was nonchalantly leaning against the wall under a life-size mural of an English fox-hunt scene, one that showed the master of the hounds raising his whip to hold the pack in check before the kill. I had to introduce myself and stand careful inspection before he would admit to being Mr. Norman; his manner had that peculiar grave courtesy of the village parson welcoming a stranger to his flock.

"I'm looking for some friends of mine," I said. "They told me I could find them here. Bald little shrimp of a guy and his wife, a big, lively blonde. Mean anything to you?"

"Do these friends of yours have names, Mr. Bailey?" No sarcasm intended, merely a polite correction of my oversight.

I stared at him and said, "Yeah, but if you can't make them for me without names I'm just wasting my time."

He nodded solemnly as if acknowledging a compliment. "Maybe you are."

"Too bad," I said. "Maybe they need me worse than I need them."

That gave him pause. He took his shoulder off the wall and his unctuous tone became thoughtful. "I'll have to ask," he said. "Might take a little while."

I told him I would stick around, and drifted over with the crowd to watch the game. At the nearest table they were playing jackpots draw, two sailors from the submarine base at Long Beach, two potbellied small-shopkeeper types, two grim-faced, bespectacled, middle-aged housewives and a stocky young Chinese girl who seemed to be winning. Action was fast enough and betting vigorous. I wondered why it didn't do a thing to me. No kick, no chills, no clenching fists, no stinging in my veins. I didn't even care who took the pot. Yet it was poker that had been the first to get me by the throat, nine years ago. . . .

"This way, please, sir."

The chip girl twittered at me like a frightened sparrow with a tomcat on its tail. Her thin, anemic body looked as if it barely managed to support the weight of the heavy green canvas change apron. I smiled for her, she needed so much to be shown I was a good guy after all, and walked behind her through the crowd and to a door between the snack bar and the armored cashier's cage, back in the rear.

She knocked, and when the buzzer catch went off she quickly stood aside and shot another of those birdlike apprehensive glances at me. "Mr. Hunter will see you now," she told me breathlessly, and almost ran away behind the clink and jingle of her stock-in-trade.

There were two adding machines, a typewriter and an old-fashioned mast-high cardboard filing cabinet. There was a battered old office desk, cleared of everything but a half-empty highball glass. There were three more doors, one in every wall, and no windows, and another bank of fluorescent lights, and a slick, shiny floor of polished green linoleum that showed the crisscross rubber-track prints of a wheelchair now drawn up behind the desk. The wheelchair's occupant came pretty near to fooling me for a second or two. He looked more like Burt Jones than Burt himself. He was older, smaller, skinnier, balder, more insignificant, his skull more perfectly egg shaped and tinted a more violent pink, his features even sulkier, worse tempered. Only the narrow, mouse gray eyes he laid on me were different, like small-gauge shotgun barrels, hard and hollow, and offensively suspicious.

"Don't know you," he informed me testily right off the bat. "You from the Riverside D.A.?" He saw my head shake. "Federal?"

"No, sir."

"A private boy scout, huh? We got no use here for your kind."

"Can't blame you, Mr. Hunter," I said pleasantly. "It happens I'm not any kind of a dick. I just dropped in for a chat with Burt and Rita. Your manager out there may not have understood."

"A friend!" he scoffed at me. "They don't make 'em, I'll tell you that much. Who do you think you're kidding, boy?"

"You must be Burt's brother," I said. "You don't need to worry, Mr. Hunter, I'm clean. If they're around they'll see me all right. It's just a question of a little information."

He took those shotgun-barrel eyes from me and sneered into his highball almost good-naturedly. "Sit down, boy," he said. "Maybe I can help you. Drink?"

"Plain Scotch, thank you. This isn't anything that would be in your line, Mr. Hunter. If your brother and his wife are not here, I'd appreciate it if you'd put me in touch."

"They tell you about this place?" He swung the wheelchair closer to the desk and stabbed a button twice. His tone wasn't exactly skeptical anymore, or even curious. He sounded like a man who had made up his mind about me. I was a bore who would have to be humored, but not very much. It was an attitude that bothered me, because I had no real remedy for it. I was already pretty sure that he had no intention of passing the ball.

"Just the address," I said carelessly. "Let's get it straight, Mr. Hunter. This is purely a social call. Nothing to sell, nothing to collect. All I'm asking is a minor favor."

The door behind me opened, not the one through which I had come in, and a man in a striped jersey T-shirt stuck in his head. Hunter scowled up at him and snapped, "Plain Scotch," and waved him off impatiently. The man grunted and left, slamming the door. Hunter showed me another of his sulky sneers.

"Sounds different now," he pointed out. "A minor favor. You told my manager you figured Burt would need you more than you'd need him."

"Why not let Burt decide?" I offered cheerfully.

He shrugged. Not in contempt, but more as if he were resigned, and prepared to be reasonable with me. "Okay, boy. If that's the way you want it. I guess he'll know where he can find you."

"You mean tonight?"

"Tonight, tomorrow, next week, what's the difference? How do I know when he's gonna turn up? You in a hurry?"

"Here we go again," I said. "Yes, I'm in a hurry, Mr. Hunter. I made a special trip down here to see your brother. I'd love to explain what this is all about, but it happens to be a strictly personal matter that doesn't concern you a bit. It wouldn't even interest you, believe me."

This time the look he gave me flickered uncertainly. He was still bored and out of sorts with me, but something had come up to puzzle him, and he wanted to count the pot before deciding to make another bet. The room was suddenly so quiet that the ribbons attached to the air-conditioning vent sounded like bunting flapping in a gale. I started losing both my patience and my nerve. It was becoming more and more obvious to me that Burt's connection with my own affairs had to be thoroughly explored without delay.

"Whatever gave you the idea the Riverside D.A. has anything to do with this?" I prodded Hunter stupidly.

His eyes lost the flicker and had buckshot behind them again. Palm Springs is in Riverside County. I realized then, about ten minutes too late, that he was mixed up in the deal himself. He had me labeled as a shakedown artist all along. The kind of wolf who preys on other wolves.

It was a nasty break, but I was stuck with it. Not even showing my real hand would do a bit of good, if I could have accepted the preposterous risk involved. Now there was nothing for it but to try to throw a scare at him, to play it tough the way he would expect.

"What's the matter?" I asked him. "Your brother a crook? Maybe the cops can find him for me quicker than you. If that's the way *you* want it."

The man in the striped jersey T-shirt came

shuffling in with my jigger of Scotch and a water chaser on a tray. He put the tray on the desk before me, grunted and shuffled out again. The door slammed, hard enough to rattle the glasses. Hunter was reaching in a drawer, came up with a box of cheap drugstore cigars. He tossed me one, and stuck another in between his thin pink lips and twisted the wheelchair back into position where he could strike a match on the wall.

"Cops," he said reflectively. "We got cops in this town, boy. The best that money can buy." Current from the air vent unraveled the long gray streamer of smoke he blew across the desk. He gazed after it dreamily, ignoring me.

"Well, fine," I said. "You haven't anything to worry about, then."

"That's right."

His complacency was worse than a deliberate insult. I climbed to my feet and broke out a snarl. "Let's see about a phone someplace around. This is a gambling joint you're running, mister. Maybe the Big Fellow up in Bel Air can talk you into giving me a little service."

He actually smiled at me, with his kind of face. This was what he'd been waiting for.

"Don't get excited, boy," he told me peacefully. "Go on, sit down and drink your drink. So you're working for the Big Fellow up in Bel Air."

"What about it?"

"Makes a difference. You ought to know. New man, aren't you?"

I didn't like that. His tone was more solicitous than sarcastic, but I didn't like it anyway. It made no sense for him to relax while I was the one to come down with a case of the jitters. The whole interview had gone sour on me from the start. There was something peculiarly wrong with it, the same queer, off-key dissonance as when the woodwind section happens to be lagging half a bar behind the brass. I could hear it, and see it, and feel it, but I couldn't reason it out or get it back into the groove, no more than anyone can explain a nightmare or influence its course. The analogy struck me as a pretty close one, because on the instant I thought of it the room started playing tricks with me. The walls were growing longer, the ceiling bulged up like a balloon and the floor acquired a sudden alarming tilt to windward. The wheelchair with Hunter in it seemed to be rapidly rolling away from me, while the desk came sliding into my ribs, almost knocking me over, and forcing me to hang on to it for support.

As nightmares go, this one did not amount to very much, but it involved all the usual sensations of blurred vision, a distant sound of roaring and a feeling of abject physical docility. It made me shake myself, like a dog in his bath, and then my lungs stopped breathing and my stomach stopped writhing and the roof of the Club Gaucho came down on me, quietly and slowly, all the way down into darkness.

11

THE TUNNEL WAS LONG, narrow and soggy wet inside, and it whirled crazily around off center like a maniac's idea of something new in the way of amusement-park attractions. There was light at the end, beamed straight down the tapering, spinning exit shaft: no more than a pinpoint at first, but swiftly growing in size and in cold white spherical brilliance. The light seemed to suck me in and force me down at the same time, exerting a concurrent drag and thrust of more than sufficient authority to leave me completely helpless.

Whatever I was using for a head felt like a red-hot cannonball, suitable for sinking the *Flying Dutchman*, not suitable for functional human employment. Yet somehow, mysteriously, it was regaining certain human faculties. It registered an offensive smell and issued a groan; it tasted blood and vomit; it picked up the exhaust gurgle of an idling motor and the gruff, uninterested mumble of voices, the sharp, metallic squawk of a radio turned up loud.

"...twenty-two, roger," the radio was saying in a stridently officious soprano. "Twenty-six, on your query: the license number is Illinois nine

Baker one one dash one five. Approach with caution, code two. Eighteen, no make. Twelve, call your station. . . ."

I groaned some more and tried to raise myself on one elbow, tried wearily to crawl out from under the inexorably impaling spotlight. A foot appeared in the beam and prodded my kidneys, not roughly, just enough to persuade me to abandon the attempt. Now I got a rat's-eye view of two pairs of legs in identical gray flannel slacks, and a glimpse of two coarsely checked tweed sports coats side by side.

"Rise and shine, Mac. Whatsa big idea, messing up our nice clean gutter, hah?"

The voice from the shadows had a thin, hard, big-city accent, neither friendly nor unfriendly but plain matter-of-fact, the kind of voice that has never learned to shout in excitement or to whisper in emotion, so that it sounds almost exactly the same in the bedroom, at a baseball game or in court. I shivered and made another formidable effort, and succeeded this time in pulling myself up into something of a hunch-backed crouch on the curb. My head was cooling down, but the sidewalk continued to reel under me, and every inch of my digestive tract was throbbing with a caustic pain. Just talking was almost as bad as swallowing a razor blade.

"What time is it?"

"You got the time on you, Clem? This guy wants to know. He don't carry a watch."

I held up my wrist for them. The watch said 10:43, but its crystal had been smashed. They didn't laugh or give me any kind of a reaction.

They just stood over me, out of the light, watching. The radio spoke up and said icily, "K.G.P.D., 11:00 P.M. All cars, clear frequency two. Forty-nine, go ahead."

"I think I can make it now, fellows," I said. "Thanks very much for standing by."

"You hear that, Clem? Guy figures he can make it now."

"You're not going to arrest me, Lieutenant, are you?" I demanded, feeling the sweat break out all over me again.

"Dettlinger," he said. "Detective Sergeant. Yeah, it's a pinch, sweetheart. Drunk and disorderly. Okay with you?"

"Listen, Sergeant, I'm not drunk. That was a Mickey they slipped me. Chloral hydrate."

Clem snickered. Dettlinger said politely, "My, what a shame. They shouldn't have done a thing like that to you. Maybe you wanna tell us how come."

"I don't know."

"Think of that. You don't know, hah, kiddo? Okay, lemme tell you. Anytime one of you syndicate mobsters gonna show his face in our territory, bingo, down comes the ax. We ain't fooling around, and we don't owe your boss no favors. Not in this town we don't. We got a judge here, he'll toss you sixty days in the morning, on the road gang, no bail. Come on, let's get going."

The radio coughed sharply and said, "Forty-nine, clear. Sixteen, to Ardmore and 186th; a woman screaming. Check disturbance, keep the peace."

I said, "For God's sake, Sergeant, this is all a

big mistake! They got the wrong impression at the poker club. I'm not a mobster for the syndicate, or do you think I'd have been square enough to drink their Scotch?''

''So far as I'm concerned,'' said Dettlinger, ''you goddamn hoods are just a bunch of jerks. Doc Hunter claims you tried to put the bite on him. He ought to know.''

''All I asked him was to let me talk to his brother.''

''Yeah? He don't have any. You putting me on, boy, or are you just plain dumb?''

Doc Hunter! *You remember what Doc said. If they catch us muscling in....* I was squirming with confusion and bewilderment, helplessly trying to match up the pieces of this crazy jigsaw pattern. Some of it made sense— dangerous, paradoxical sense. The knockout drops, for one example, had been ordered for me long before I'd made a nuisance of myself. They'd been expecting me at the Club Gaucho— they knew my name and they had been warned about me in advance, warned that I was Walter Hitchcock's errand boy. Burt Jones himself must have tipped them off. Whatever he'd been up to in Palm Springs, I was the party who'd unwittingly scared him away. They had concluded that I knew too much and that I meant to squeeze a payoff out of them. *New man, aren't you?*

''So all right, I'm dumb,'' I said. ''But if Doc has no brother, who's this character that looks like him, the way one rotten egg looks like another? The one who drags a girdle full of blonde around with him. Tell me that much, Sergeant, will you please?''

The two of them stiffened a little as if they were mildly surprised. It was quiet again for several seconds; even the radio released no more than a drone and a sputter of static. From the ocean a low bank of cool, salty fog came leisurely rolling down the narrow side street. At last Dettlinger demanded roughly, ''If you're no hood, then what's your grift here, Mac?''

''No grift. This fellow and his wife, they asked me to come down and look them up.''

It was Clem who obliged with another snicker. Dettlinger snapped his fingers, loud enough to sound like a .22 going off. ''Let's see your driver's license.''

He studied it for quite a while. This time I got a profile view of him, straw hat brim pulled way down into deep-socket eyes, the cynical prow of a nose, the mustache bristle camouflaging full, almost weakly sensual lips, the rock-hard chin jutting out belligerently into the light. My license was three years old, and it still showed the Normandie Apartments, which is a pretty fair Los Feliz District address.

''You work for a living?''

''Musician.''

''Got a union ticket on you that says so?''

I pretended to search my wallet. The spotlight beam caught a flash of my old Army ID card. He snatched it out of my hands, glanced at it and pushed it back at me.

''Burt Jorgenson,'' he said, half to himself. ''Him and the floozie been roping for Doc's

private back-room game again. Some kind of
cousins, I hear. You better get wise to yaself,
soldier.''

"How's that?"

"You hear him, Clem? This guy don't know the
score." His tone acquired the contemptuous
benevolence he would have put into it while sup-
plying directions to a kid on an unfamiliar
newspaper route. "Look, soldier, poker's legal
here in California, but only where the city coun-
cil says it is. The law kinda passes the buck to the
people, see? They should figure it out for
themselves, do they wanna call it a game of skill
or what. In Formosa we've opened her up six
months ago, and that makes us and maybe two,
three other towns up north the only places
where a cop can't make much of a living anymore. Doc's club's all square, on account of we
keep it that way, but I don't advise nobody to get
mixed up in none of them private parties like he
organizes on the side. You got a car?''

"Yes, of course."

"Okay, get lost. Stay off our reservation. I dun-
no who let you out after dark in the first place."

They were gone in a sudden hot rush of exhaust smoke, the radio's strident cackle trailing
in their wake until after they'd turned the block.
I struggled to my feet and staggered away from
there in the opposite direction, away from the
ocean's distant angry rumble, back to Main
Street and past the endless parking line to where
the Ford was waiting, meekly jammed between
the bumpers of two other rusty wrecks.

It took me five minutes of torture to batter

myself out of hock, and by the time I hit the freeway going north it became pretty obvious that I wasn't going to make it back to Palm Springs, or at least not all in one piece. Chloral hydrate is tricky stuff—it plays hell with your coordination. I must have thrown most of it off being sick in the gutter, but driving was largely still a matter of wobbling and weaving all over the road, like learning to ride a bicycle. There were stretches of a hundred yards at a time where I couldn't even see where I was going, and moments when I had to slam the brakes on in the middle of the center lane, to be sick some more, out the window to leeward. There were various sorts of funny buzzing noises, and weird whistling noises, and delusions about swarms of multicolored fireflies spattering on my windshield. Then an arm or a leg would check out for a spell and would have to be deliberately called back to order, usually by punishing the numb spots with a fist.

I got off the freeway somehow and made a wrong turn without being aware of it. Whatever twilight instincts will stay on the job in such a situation guided me through the late-supper traffic out on Wilshire Boulevard. I woke up with a sudden start to find myself slewed half across the driveway curb in front of Marion's apartment house. Pablo, the elevator jockey, leaned in over the wheel and was slapping my face and hissing at me in almost comical distress.

"Yes, sir, yes, sir! I go fetch doctor, Mr. Bailey. You just keep still, yes, sir." He saw me stare and shake my head. "Cops chasing you that shot you up, Mr. Bailey?'' he pressed me, and his cocky sparrow eyes were big and round.

"No cops," I mumbled. "No doctor. Go 'way, lea' me 'lone."

"Gee, you look pretty awful, Mr. Bailey," he assured me solemnly. "You ain't just plastered up, are you? Your shirt's all over blood, yes, sir."

I roused myself enough to muster a growl. "Beat it. Thish isn't any of your businesh. Business. For crying out loud, why can't you let me sit here for a little while?"

"Dontcha want to go up, Mr. Bailey?" He was studying me now with an air of quizzical perplexity, like a robin with a nestful of cuckoo's young.

"I'll be all right. I didn't mean to come here in the first place. You wanna help, get thish heap off shidewalk. *Sidewalk....*"

"Yes, sir, yes, sir."

He shoved my feet from the pedals and slid in beside me. The Ford backed up and puttered smoothly down the driveway ramp into the sepulchral white cement cavern of the basement garage. I dozed off again while he parked it, and didn't wake up until the elevator door snarled open on the sixth-floor landing. He'd managed somehow to drag me out of the car and prop me up on the floor of the elevator.

"Hey, jus' a minute! Take me down!"

He neatly blocked my lunge at the controls. "I phone Miss Faraday. First she give me hell, then she tell me to bring you up, yes, sir."

Marion came sweeping down the hall in a rustle of baby-blue kimono silk. Her face was still glistening with cold cream, but she'd wielded a lipstick and hurriedly tied a scarf around her curlers.

"Oh, Rick, *really*! Are you out of your mind? What in God's name has happened to you now?"

They were both of them pulling at me like two small tugs attempting to dock a fractious ocean liner. I shook them off and wandered dizzily into the apartment and sat down on the davenport, swaying with the breeze. There was excited whispering behind my back, and then the door slammed shut and Marion came flouncing past me on a beeline for the liquor cabinet. I fought off a shudder and caught the hem of her negligee, just in time.

"Coffee," I croaked. "Strong black coffee. Lots of it."

"Oh, all right."

She shied away from me into the kitchenette. I made it to the bathroom, not quite on all fours, and sat on the tiles struggling out of my filthy clothes, and crawled under the shower like a dog. The rush of cold water blacked me out again before it whipped my blood back into circulation.

I was fixing the cut on my chin with a Band-Aid when Marion stuck her head around the door. "Your old suit's on the bed," she informed me coldly. "You left it here last Monday, in a package. I pressed it for you."

Thanking her sounded a little silly. I succeeded in making myself halfway presentable again and in navigating back to the living room under my own steam. My head was still throbbing and my eyes were still playing tricks on me, but I knew the coffee would take care of that. The coffee was waiting for me, boiling in the percolator, strong enough to wrestle a grizzly bear. It raced through my system like a dose of cauterizer burning out the dross.

She watched me from the couch; she sat very straight with her head held high, the folds of her kimono decorously arranged. She had wiped off the cold cream, and fluffed out her long blond curls and organized herself. Now I was getting the silent treatment, the level, expressionless stare, the full red lips compressed in a straight, disapproving line. I poured myself a third large breakfast cup and lighted a cigarette with hands that were almost useful again. It didn't seem as if there was anything to say, anywhere to look.

"Are you sure you don't need a doctor?"

"Quite sure."

"It might be concussion or something."

"I know what it is. This stuff will fix it."

There was another longish pause. Down the block on Wilshire the banshee scream of an ambulance went by like a streak of lightning. The kitchen refrigerator turned itself on with a sudden high-pitched whine.

"I told you you'd be back pretty soon," she said at last, quietly and with no hint of complacency in her tone.

There was nothing I could say to that, either, so I let it hang in the air between us. The city had a hundred thousand rooms, that night and every night, in which a man and a woman were confronting each other and leaving words and sentences to hang in the air between them. Maybe there should be a law.

"You might as well tell me. About the fight."

"It wasn't."

"Oh, Rick, don't be childish."

"I'm not. Just a slight misunderstanding. They threw me out. The cut is where I slipped on the pavement."

"Were you gambling?"

"No."

She sighed, and the warm hazel eyes flickered dangerously. "I suppose there was a woman involved. . . ."

I matched the sigh and set my teeth. My reaction was meaningless, automatic, an ancient rite all men have performed and all women have expected through the ages of history, whenever that subject was brought up. I didn't get any kind of charge out of it. The night's events had drained me of emotion.

"No woman," I said dully. "It's much more involved than that."

"Oh. Is it?"

She rose impulsively and came over to sit on the arm of my chair. Her long, slender, capable hand touching my cheek brought me a faint bitter-almond scent of Jergens Lotion. "Darling. . . why can't you be sensible and quit acting like a neurotic playboy? If you'd only take a grip on yourself, get a job, start all over again fresh. Rick, you could lick the world, don't you realize that?"

"Rule number three," I said. "When the animal shows signs of being depressed, feed his ego."

"Must you be cynical on top of everything?"

she flamed, and just as quickly subsided into con-
trition. "I'm sorry, darling. But you know yourself how you always come to me when you're in
trouble. Isn't it logical, then, that if we were
married you'd never be in trouble at all? Can't
you see where that proves we belong together?"

"You don't understand," I said. "It wouldn't
work. I wish I thought it would."

I could feel her wince, but she kept silent for a
while and went on rubbing the back of my neck
absentmindedly. When she spoke at last, her
voice had a funny little catch in it, as if the situation had moved an inch or two from under her
control.

"Rick, who is she?"

"Huh?"

"Please don't lie to me. Any woman can tell."

"Stop kidding yourself with that bunk. They
can't, either. They just think they can. This is
something else altogether."

"Then you've got to explain."

"I can't. It's not my secret."

She slipped off my chair and walked over to
the fireplace for a cigarette from the box on the
shelf, striking the match before I could get up to
serve her, and holding the flame cupped in her
hands, like a man. She appeared relaxed, almost
vindictively satisfied, leaning back against the
mantelpiece, smoking thoughtfully in long, slow
drags. "At least you could let me in on where
you've been all this time since Monday," she suggested carelessly.

It may have been the drug or its aftereffects
that scoured my perceptions and afforded me a

bright flash of memory. I was sixteen years old, and I'd sneaked out of our hotel suite in Boston as soon as she left for the auditorium. That was the night they'd had to cancel her concert, because of the fire backstage, and when I came home she was waiting for me, leaning against the mantelpiece, still wearing the dramatic white satin formal that made her look like a golden-haired angel. *But, Rick, where were you?* Carelessly, yes, as in a rippling arpeggio of the strings up to high F, touched off lightly by slender, skillfully caressing fingers. And in the morning she'd seen to it that the management dismissed the girl. . . .

"Darling, what's wrong?"

For the first time she appeared genuinely alarmed. I came up for air and forced my eyes back into focus.

"Don't worry. You just reminded me of my mother. The good old silver cord and all that stuff. All right, I'll tell you this much. I'm supposed to be doing a job, no kidding. They're paying me money and it's nothing illegal, but the deal happens to be very definitely under wraps. If I showed you any cards it might be very dangerous for both of us."

"Who are they? Mr. Hitchcock?" She saw me shake my head and frowned at me in quick vexation. "There, you see? I never know when to believe you. At least *he* wouldn't be dangerous to work for."

I didn't even want to laugh. "Never mind, skip it. This thing is bound to fall through as it is. All it

amounts to is a college boy in some kind of jam.
I'll be on it a few more days, maybe.''

"You sound like a private detective or something just as nasty,'' she said disdainfully. ''And
you still haven't told me where you've been all
this while, or how you got into a fight.''

"Sorry.''

"Oh, Rick, *honestly* . . . .''

I got up on my two big feet and tested the floor.
It felt steady again, not as if this were opening
night at the Starlight Roof. "What more do you
want me to say? I can't sit here arguing about it
all night.''

"You're not thinking of leaving?''

"Of course. I've got to.''

She took her shoulders off the mantelpiece and
came sailing into me in a burst of angry tears, a
flurry of silk and scented skin and clawing nails.
The idea seemed to be that I was too sick to go
out, but not sick enough to escape a wrestling
match. She nearly succeeded in pinning my
shoulders to the mat on her first wild rush, and
for a minute or so we were locked in a struggle
that knocked over several assorted pieces of furniture, brought down two pictures from the
walls and wound up on the davenport in pretty
much of a draw. There is nothing funny about
fighting a woman: it makes you feel stupid and
clumsy and horribly mixed up. I even began
wanting her all over again, almost mechanically,
or from sheer force of animal habit, or because of
something that would have caused Dr. Hirsch to
purse his lips.

"I'm going. All through?''

"No! No, no, no. You can't. I won't let you."

"I can. I will."

"Darling. Kiss me!"

I tore loose an arm and struck out blindly. The blow caught her high on the cheek and she sagged under me, instantly limp and peaceful and wearily asleep. I squirmed off the couch and stood watching her, biting my knuckles, leaning into wave after wave of black remorse. Then the fridge in the kitchen switched off with a click like the cocking of a gun and made me bolt from the apartment in a crazy headlong rush, down six flights of stairs into the basement garage and up the driveway ramp, down to Wilshire and east once more as fast as the clattering old Ford would carry me away.

12

THE RAIN STARTED at Alhambra. It kept on coming for the next seventy-five miles, sometimes no worse than a hazy drizzle, sometimes in sudden impetuous torrents. They swamped the windshield wipers and turned the highway into a blur of shallow, racing water, soaking up the feeble yellow glare of my headlights.

It was just the kind of trip to kill or cure a man with a hole in his head. It didn't do either for me, but a couple of hours of fighting the wheel, the road and the elements will usually take your mind off your troubles. By 2:30 A.M. on the dashboard clock I was cold, tired, sober and doing sixty miles an hour through Cabazon, which is where the desert takes over and the clouds pile up in helpless frustration against the towering crest of the San Jacinto range. Here the rain stopped dead in its tracks and the sky was swept clear as if by a single stroke of some gigantic broom. Where the canyon's narrow defile broke through, the night acquired a sudden tropical brilliance of velvet and gold, and the temperature rose twenty degrees. It was late enough for the evening wind to have blown itself out, but on the road my tires changed tune from a whistle to a dry, gritty wheeze through the drifting sands.

Palm Springs was still a carnival of neon signs and jukebox music. The Biltmore garden shimmered in a flutter of Chinese lanterns where couples in period costume were dancing on the lawn to the frenzied strings of a Gypsy band. The smell of money was heavy in the air, mixed with the scent of women and the fumes of high-test gasoline. Together they easily overrode the cloying aroma of the sagebrush.

I bullied through four miles of traffic and picked up the highway again at the edge of town, where it veered away from the somber bastion of the mountains and plunged south into the valley, between the country clubs, the dude ranches, the flossy motor courts and the last few blocks of privately supported white stucco caravansaries. Most of these were in darkness and silence, but halfway around a familiar-looking greasewood copse there was light and noise again. My feet came down hard on the pedals before I consciously recognized the place.

For five minutes or so I sat staring at it from the shoulder of the road, brooding like a pickpocket at a nudist camp. *Get wise to yourself, soldier....* That was all right, that part of it. By that time I knew which way the dice were loaded. I didn't want Lorna to be there. Not because of the job I was supposed to do, but because I wanted to believe in her. I wanted her to be what she seemed to be, not what a detective agency or a file clerk in an airline office claimed she was.

I got out of the car and started walking.

The light came from a square of baby arcs mounted on tall steel poles to illuminate the patio. The noise was a composite of shouting and laughter, the splash of water from the pool and the booming of a stereo system going all out with the Rolling Stones. That much intelligence was easily available as far as the mouth of the driveway, but it needed a regular jungle patrol to fill in the sketch. There were picket fences, barbed-wire fences, hedges of ironwood and jacaranda, honeysuckle bushes ten feet high and cactus patches big enough to stop a cattle stampede. I threshed around in there for quite some little spell and never got much closer to the patio than hand grenade distance. That allowed me to confirm that a party was going on, but not to identify the guests.

It was the sort of situation in which you've got a choice: drop out of the pot or bet the limit on a pair of deuces. I cut back to the driveway and hung around flexing my pride for a while, and marched right on up to the front porch of Mr. Alfredo Vanni's elegant Monterey villa. Two dozen cars lined the courtyard circle, but the small yellow Buick coupé failed to catch my eye until the very instant I leaned a thumb on the button of the doorbell chimes.

The yellow Buick confused me. It was exactly where I might have expected to find it, but it confused me anyway. It had never occurred to me that the Joneses might not, after all, have been scared away. They had simply checked out at the Hacienda to save the bill for a night's lodging.... It followed that whatever they were after was just about to blow up in my face. The notion was one I couldn't use at all. I almost decided on the spot to pull out again. I simply wasn't prepared to meet that much more of a raise.

The butler was coughing discreetly in my ear. He had quietly opened the door behind me, opened it far enough to let him look me over and no more. His face had a slightly pained expression showing me he didn't approve of what he saw. He was a small, wrinkled, elderly black dressed up in black tie and brass-button tails. They had probably found him wandering around the old plantation set of *Gone with the Wind* on the Selznick back lot.

"Calling on Mr. Vanni," I said with a lump in my throat.

"No reporters, suh."

Inspiration sprang alive in my weary mind like a freshly sown dragon's tooth. "That's right," I said. "No reporters, and don't you forget it, my friend. That's just what I've come to see him about. Bailey's the name, Globe International Pictures, publicity staff. Tell him it's urgent, but get him aside before you mention any names. I don't want to disturb the guests."

He wasn't happy, but I'd struck a note of casual insistence that scored with him. He squirmed a little in his boots and peered at me over the gold-plated rims of his spectacles, and reluctantly opened the door another sixteen inches. That put me in the hall, on the mangy lion skin that served as a doormat, and with two magnificent stands of Spanish conquistador armor for company. The butler apparently intended to leave me there, so I pushed past him and barged on ahead through the most likely-looking archway.

This was the room all right, a thousand square feet of gleaming blond parquet featuring two bleached-maple Bechstein concert grands, a built-in music library and a huge carved-oak Renaissance desk that belonged in there about as much as a Sherman tank would belong in the Battle of Agincourt. One wall displayed a full-length canvas of a carousing Flemish peasant girl in the Rubens school; another was covered from ceiling to floor with blowups of opera singers and movie stars, all female and all of them fondly autographed. The French doors and the picture window next to them had forest-green velvet portieres carefully drawn together. Behind them were the booming stereo, and the splashing, and the rest of the big clambake.

This time it was easy—split the curtains at a crack and get yourself an eyeful. They'd have you believe that those Hollywood parties at three in the morning are commonly run in a style that would curl the hair of any character in *Quo Vadis*. Out here we know a little more of what we can expect. I counted twenty-one people, some of them with faces equally familiar to the president of France and to the average Arab peasant. Three couples were dancing, two in formal evening dress, the other in bathing suits. Four hardy souls were disporting themselves in the pool, tossing a plastic beach ball around with a great deal of unsophisticated hilarity. The remaining eleven made up one table of contract bridge and three of gin rummy. They appeared to be completely absorbed in a common effort of grim concentration on the cards, in blank defiance of the racket going on around them.

There was no sign of Lorna Ryan anywhere on deck.

The butler came in view and stood hovering over the nearest gin table. I'd been watching that table with a certain amount of wry amusement. It neatly solved the problem of what kind of badger game the Joneses were playing. Steve Kovacs's contemptuous warning rasped in my ears. *Meester Vanni iss one beeg spender.... We do not mess with Meester Vanni. Iss bad for beezness.*

The butler was whispering now, and getting the lifted eyebrow, the sweeping gesture of impatient scorn. I dropped the curtains and backed away from the window—there would be a slight delay, a little kicking of heels, at least long enough for them to finish the hand. A studio publicity man, or flack, as the trade press calls him, swings about as much social respect as the second assistant janitor in the prop department. He may function in any capacity down the line, from father confessor to whipping boy, but he'll never see the day when someone holds still for him in the middle of a hand of gin.

I sank into a monk's cloth-covered armchair facing the painting on the wall. The bosomy peasant wench ogled me lecherously, offering her tankard at a tilt that spilled a runnel of scarlet muscadine. I caught myself staring at her and forced the sluggishly turning wheels in my mind back into gear.

At least I wouldn't have to fret about the Joneses anymore. They were trespassing all right, but not on my property. I wondered now whatever I'd been thinking of to get excited over them. It meant nothing to me, the way they'd roped themselves a mark who seemed to enjoy being taken for a ride across the board. It was, after all, only money—the guy would spend it somewhere, on the ponies, at chemin de fer, or in the slots at Vegas. He might as well lose it in a game of gin at fifty bucks a point.

The only member of the firm who would be taking a chance there was Doc Hunter. Milking the pigeons in syndicate territory sounded to me like a pretty unhealthy idea. But then Doc might be relying entirely on the local fix. The town of Formosa had certainly seemed as carefully buttoned up as they come. Maybe he could afford to relax in there, and indulge in occasional raids on the icebox, such as this one.

I didn't think he could, or that it mattered one way or the other.

What mattered was how they'd found out about Lorna. It was the only part I didn't like. But gamblers setting up a kill will often spend a lot of time and effort scouting the mark in advance, finding out all about his background, his habits and his friends, the way a burglar will case the joint. If that was it, then Burt and Rita probably did know the answer, had known all along. They'd been staying at the Hacienda del Sol for several days before I ever arrived on the scene,

and so had Lorna; the days the Big Fellow up in
Bel Air had needed to get a line on me and rub
my nose into the job. . . .

"Signor Bailey?"

The *signor* part was strictly for laughs—my
host appeared to be in something of a jocular
mood. He had sneaked up on me through the
archway behind my back and now he stood smil-
ingly watching me in a typical singer's pose, leaning into the crook of one of the Bechsteins, one
hand pocketed, the other freely available for
gesticulation. He was even shorter, portlier than
I remembered him from the casino the night
before. Perhaps it was the dinner jacket with the
fancy cummerbund in royal-blue satin, and the
broad, theatrical lapels. But the smile had more
cigar than teeth in it, a cautious smile that was
prepared to accept me only against its owner's
better judgment.

"I think we meet before," he said slowly, and
his accent was almost imperceptible.

"Sure, when you cleaned me out last night," I
said with a grin. "Quite a coincidence. Don't get
me wrong, Mr. Vanni. Globe didn't send me
down to keep tabs on you here in Palm Springs."

"Ah-ha!" This time he gave me a better
glimpse of the dental work. "But you are from
the publicity, eh, my friend? That is, as you say,
quite a coincidence. Why do you come crash my
party at such an hour, if you please?"

"I wouldn't have. Not without a pretty good
reason."

"Okay, fine. You explain to me, eh?"

I nodded and deliberately stalled him off by

lighting a cigarette in slow motion. I'd made up my mind that he wasn't the only ham in the world who could read a line and sing a song.

"Hollywood called me out of bed," I said. "Told me to rush right over and get a statement from you. Looks like you might be in a spot, Mr. Vanni."

Now I had his ear. The elaborate snap of the fingers, the pouting lower lip were supposed to convey his opinion of the studio's judgment, not of mine. This was the sort of deal he had learned to expect from the jittery front-office bosses in the picture industry. It put me in the clear; he wouldn't have dreamed of blaming the flunky, or suspecting his motives.

"Santa Maria, is always same t'ing!" His accent was back on duty, from sheer good nature. "Somebody lose-a nerve, raise beeg fuss over notting. Send-a man to Vanni, take statement. Okay, you tell em, whatsa wrong?"

"You won't like this," I said carefully. "Rona Barrett's on the warpath, and she's after your scalp."

"Pouff! I like verree much. My scalp she's fixed up pretty good, eh?" He patted his sleekly pomaded jet black coiffure approvingly.

"You could always buy a new one," I said. "But you can't laugh off a lady who raises hell and fireflies every day in four hundred newspapers and twice a week on a major network. This time she's on another of those clean-up-the-movies crusades, and she's loaded for bear, where you're concerned. It's pure dumb luck that one of us happened to catch her at Ma

Maison and fed her a bottle. Now we've got till
noon tomorrow if we're going to beat her dead-
line, and you'd better have all the right answers,
Mr. Vanni. Remember the girl we tested last year
at your suggestion?"

The romantic hazel eyes were round and puzzled now. "*Si, si*, Mees Ryan. I remember. . . ."

"Rona dug up that you paid for her passage
from New York."

He stared at me, his hand with the cigar in it
frozen in midair. From the patio the shouting and
splashing of the beach-ball players seemed suddenly to come in much more noisily. The stereo
was obliging with an album by The Who.

"But of course I pay. Costs money to fly—no
pay, no ticket."

"Ever hear about the Mann Act?"

That did it. He was Rigoletto and I was Spara-
fucile, showing him the dirk. "Santa Maria,
what-a you doing to me? These Mann Act, it is for
white slavery, eh? Whatsamatta, you t'ink Vanni
is-a pimp?"

"Oh, come now," I said. "Don't you know it's
a federal rap anytime you pay the freight across a
state line for the lady friend?"

"Hah! Why you t'ink Mees Ryan my lady
friend, eh?"

"They don't pay me to think," I said. "I'm just
telling you what we're up against with Rona Barrett."

He let go with a few choice bits of Italian on the
subject of crusading gossip columnists. I merely
got the drift of it, but it seemed to relieve his
feelings no end. When he came back to me at last

the accent was almost purged again, and his tone almost cagey. "She's my niece, my late sister's *figlietta....*"

"That's better. If we can make that stick, we'll spike the deal."

"Okay. You spike 'im."

"We'll need to fill it in a little more."

"How you mean, fill it in?"

"The details," I said patiently. "Just so we'll have the picture straight, in confidence. Enough of it to make Rona lay off."

He scowled at me, reluctantly digesting the idea. "Okay, but no good for publicity, you understand. My sister, she run away from home in Milano, Italy. Black hoofer with a Yankee vaudeville troupe. Was a big disgrace, big scandal, twenty years ago when I am still a *comprimario* at La Scala. She never marry the guy, or anyway I never hear. But ten years later, when I am already star at Metropolitan, comes a letter from mother superior, a convent school in Baltimore. Is confidential, very 'ush-'ush. I make a visit, and she tells me my sister gone, catch pneumonia years ago, she's got the *fanciulla* in school but no more money, this guy Ryan disappear before she ever born. Okay, so Vanni pays, you understand."

He was actually going through the motions of a bank teller counting out the scratch. I forced a grin of sympathy and said, "Go on, you're doing fine. This is the stuff we need."

"Is not much more. She leaves school at eighteen, I pull strings in New York, I fix up job. Pretty girl, makes nice model, very respectable, lotsa nice clothes, good times. I explain situation, she catch on quick, very discreet, very sensible. I tell her Vanni takes care of her until she's twenty-one. After that, chickie, you're on your own."

"You give her an allowance, is that it?"

"Yes, nice girl, needs more money to live on than she can make. Be twenty-one next month, maybe get married pretty soon. Tries out in pictures, I coach her, no damn good. Makes a nice model, not a movie star. Girl's gotta be a bitch to go places in pictures—no bitch, no can act. You understand."

"You know anything for sure about marriage plans?" I asked. "Because in that case it would help a lot if we could show that she's engaged right now."

He threw up his hands at me; he was getting a little tired of the deal. "She never tells me nothing. Whatsamatta you ask her yourself?"

"You don't want us to quote you on this, do you?" I said, blinking at him in surprise.

"No, no, no! I tell you already, all very discreet, very confidential. But publicity man from the studio, okay, you not shy, you can ask a young lady a question, eh?"

It was that simple, and that much of a farce. Of course I'd been fairly sure all along that he had no idea about Stu Hitchcock. It suddenly occurred to me that up to now I might not even have decanted the cream of the jest. Eve Garand's tart commentary flashed back through my mind. *Oh, Lorna has this young whipper-snapper on a string who considers himself*

*engaged to her. . . . She'll know better than to get
stuck with him.* Maybe the Big Fellow had, after
all, taken far too much for granted; maybe his
son's colossal arrogance had fooled him and
made him jump the gun. *Does a fly want sugar?* I
almost laughed out loud. The irony of such a pos-
sibility was very nearly irresistible.

"Could you tell me where we might get in
touch with your niece, Mr. Vanni?"

The shrug he gave me went all the way up to
the ceiling.

"I no see in two weeks. She gotta her own
place in Beverly Hills. It's in the phone book."

He did not even know she was here in Palm
Springs. Somehow it seemed impossible that he'd
slip in a joker on me at this point. It struck me
that I liked the guy—wanted to shake hands with
him and pat him on the back and tell him he was
beautiful. I felt good about him and everybody
else, including by all means one Walter Hitchcock, who appealed to me now as something just
short of a churlish and very much misunderstood
Santa Claus.

"Well, thanks a bunch," I said. "I think this
will be satisfactory for now. We can take it from
there, Mr. Vanni."

"Okay, fine. You take 'im." His hands picked it
up, whatever it was, and dumped it in my lap
ceremoniously. His smile knocked me silly; I
never saw the hint of mockery that must have
twisted it a little. He actually threw an arm
around my shoulder, showing me out through the
hall, a publicity man who had crashed his party
at three o'clock in the morning. It didn't look

right anymore to let him go back to the Joneses at fifty bucks a point.

"About last night," I said, hanging onto the front doorknob. "I hope you realize your friends are on the grift."

He got that one all right. "*Sí, sí,* I know. We play some more tonight. All finished now."

"They squeeze you?"

"Sure, they squeeze me. One hundred and eighty t'ousand dollars!" It was such a good gag he had to poke me in the ribs.

I stared at him. The damage was a lot worse than I had expected. "Do you mean to say you put up with that much of a boost?"

"Sure, make out check, okay, is like money in bank. Everybody 'appy."

The way he was chuckling about it, he had to have an angle. But I couldn't help running it into the ground. "For God's sake, man, that's highway robbery! You can't afford to let them get away with it!"

"They no rob me. I tell 'em maybe I better call up the Big Fellow. You are gambling man, Signor Bailey, you know who takes care of games in California. Vanni good customer, ask simple question, no harm done, everybody 'appy. I tell 'em that, and the woman she tears up my check, you understand?"

13

JOE CORNERO sounded sleepy and skeptical when I called him on the house phone on Friday morning at nine.

"Yeah, we got horses," he allowed. "A whole corral of 'em we got, and they all need a workout, that's for sure. Them old battle-axes that live here ain't exactly Gene Autry. You want me to go with you, Mr. Bailey?"

"Not this time, Joe, thanks just the same," I said. "You could lend me some leather, though, and a Stetson, if you've anything handy in my size. How about wrangling these noble steeds of yours over to my bungalow in half an hour?"

"Be glad to," he assured me carelessly, and caught his breath. "Huh? You want two of 'em?"

"That's right."

He didn't ask me who; he had a pair of eyes in his head. His whistle told me I'd be sorry. "Where you going, Mr. Bailey?"

"You're the director of recreation."

"Yeah, but you got to do your part. Well, shucks, I guess you better try Sapphire Canyon, if it's privacy you want. It's kind of nice up there, and the tourist crowd don't know about it."

"How do I get there?"

"Aw, that's easy. I'll give you Prince—he'll take you up and back if you just let him have his head. The trail ain't bad and I've marked it myself with piles of quartz just in case. Want me to pack you some lunch?"

"I guess we'll need it."

He hung up without quite laughing at me. I didn't mind—he was my friend, he could laugh at me all he liked. Outside my bedroom window the sun, and the lawn, and the birds in the olive tree seemed to be amused with me, too. The boy from room service accepted his tip with a knowing smirk. I grinned right back at him and loaded up on breakfast in a hurry and breezed into a clean blue sport shirt and a pair of slacks. I'd barely finished shaving when the clop-clop of hooves came at my back door.

"Where's the lady, Mr. Bailey?"

He was wearing tennis whites, climbing off a fat and sad-eyed pinto pony and patting its withers. He clapped his own hat on my head and handed me a pair of fancy high-heeled cow-puncher boots. I slid my stockinged feet into them and said, "Haven't asked her yet."

"I figured she'd wanna ride sidesaddle, but the tack room's fresh out of 'em," he told me, enjoying himself. "Huh? You ain't asked her?"

"No, but I'm fixing to." I inspected the nervous little sorrel mare he'd brought along for her and turned away toward the cottage next door. I saw him staring after me as if he were convinced I'd lost my mind. That didn't bother me, either. This was my day to break the bank.

The blinds were still down; a girl needs her beauty sleep. I banged on the casement, good and loud, and announced in ringing tones of doom that the British were coming. Lights snapped on inside, and a sulky little voice admonished me to go away.

"I won't. We're going on a picnic."

The bedsprings protested briefly and she came padding across the rug, lifted a single slat in the blinds to peer out at me in my Stetson and boots. One of the horses nickered thirty feet away, where Joe was straining his big ears.

"Oh, Rick, really . . . !"

"All set. Just hop into your jeans and we'll be off. Don't keep the nice man waiting."

"But I can't! I don't want to!"

"Sure you do. We'll have a lot of fun."

"I haven't even had my breakfast."

"Oh, yeah? My spies tell me you never take any. Come on, hurry up. Papa knows best."

She dropped the slat, but she didn't budge from behind the blinds. "I'm not coming," she told me defiantly. "You'd better ask somebody else."

"Young woman," I said, "if you're not on that horse in three minutes flat, I'll be right in to get you. We'll have some discipline around this joint."

"You wouldn't. . . ." But she padded away, and the lock of the bathroom door clicked shut. The shower started with a swish. I licked the grin off my lips and leaned against the wall, scuffing holes in the dust like any drugstore cowboy waiting for his girl. She took a little more than three minutes, but when she appeared on the porch there was a touch of meekness about her, in spite of the custom-tailored Levi's, silk bandanna, pure white castor hat and silver-plated riding crop.

"Do I look all right?" It sounded as if she really wanted to know.

"The general effect," I said, "is very fetching." It was hard to suppress the inflection of excitement, and she glanced at me quickly before she suddenly became preoccupied with daubing a handful of suntan cream on her pretty face.

Joe Cornero said, "Morning, miss. Betsy's a bit skittish this morning. Think you can handle her?" His square, heavy professional trainer's mug was expressionless; it startled me to realize that he disapproved of her more than incidentally. She gave him a cool little smile and waited for him to hold the stirrup before she swung into the saddle with a lissome gracefulness of movement. The sorrel looked around at her, its nostrils quivering, and danced aside a step or two, then abruptly lifted its heels. I made a grab for the reins, but she was calmly leaning back against the pitch and correcting the animal with hardly more than a touch of her knees.

"Hey, hey, you didn't pick that up in Central Park," Cornero said, visibly disappointed.

I laughed at him and climbed aboard the pinto. From the bedroom window of the bungalow next door came the sudden shrill tinkle of the telephone. I hastily reached out and slapped the fractious Betsy smartly on the crupper.

"Hiyo, Silver...!"

We were half a mile away and cantering briskly

side by side across the desert's gaudy carpet of flowers when she spoke at last.

"That was my phone, wasn't it?"

"Was it?"

"You know perfectly well."

"Maybe it was. But I had to do something quick to get you away from that old ladies' home back there."

She shot me another dubious glance and touched two slender fingers to the suntan cream on her cheeks. Her nails were long and glossy with a triple coating of red carnation polish. "Mr. Biedermayer will be furious," she said complacently. "I can't understand it, you know. For a photographer, he's always been rather punctual on these jobs, and it's costing the hotel people a hundred dollars a day just to have me around, not counting my cottage they could rent to somebody else."

I let that one go with the wind. I had every intention of telling her the whole sordid story and throwing myself upon the mercy of the court. She'd be indignant at first, and incredulous, and helplessly disgusted with me. Then I'd make it clear to her somehow what she meant to me— how badly I needed her, and what risk I was taking, and *why* I had told her about it. I'd remind her that now Bermuda was out, and neither of us could safely return to Hollywood or even stay on the coast at all: the Big Fellow would lose too much face, he couldn't afford to put up with us anymore. We'd have to pull stakes and go East where we came from. We'd make out all right. I could probably talk the union and the booking agency into giving me another chance. It was different now; she'd made a new man out of me.

All these things I really believed, as much as I was sure she'd understand and take me up on them. We would get married that same evening, on our way through Arizona. I had it all figured out, with no idea of any possible hitch. There was nothing whimsical about it to me, no pipe-dream stuff. I was sold on the deal and satisfied that I could sell her just as easily. The little matter of logic didn't enter into it in any way; it was all quite simple and natural and right, like breathing. The wheel was fixed and we were playing with the house.

Already the mountains were closing in, and rounding a grove of cottonwoods and tamarisk I picked up the first marker, an inconspicuous little heap of glittering quartz in the bend of the trail where it split into the rolling green foothills. The horses bore left without hesitation and slowed down to a trot as if by common consent. There were not so many flowers now, and the smell of sagebrush and creosote grew more pungent. The sun had rectified much of its early-morning slant. I dug out a handkerchief and cheerfully mopped up the sweat.

"Where are we going?"

I told her where and she nodded gravely. "Oh, yes. Eve mentioned it to me. She's been there."

"Alone?"

"Of course. She went to look for the lost mine. She heard the Indians around here tell about a daring young paleface who captured the daughter of a tribal chief and fled with her into the hills. They found a big sapphire and lots of other precious stones, somewhere down the canyon, but the discovery delayed their flight and the braves caught up with them and burned them at the stake. But it all happened hundreds and hundreds of years ago, the Indians say. Isn't that a wonderful story?''

"It needs a switch," I protested. "The ending isn't box office."

"Silly. Anyway, Eve says it's all symbolic, about the jewels and everything. You'll see."

The trail crossed a dry arroyo and forked again, one branch curving off around the mountain, the other tapering sharply into a single craggy defile that seemed to run smack into the rocks. There was another small pile of quartz to mark this apparent dead end. The pinto edged forward and eagerly took the lead. Where the towering cliffside rose to block our progress, a narrow passage between two formidable boulders offered unexpected access to the canyon's mouth, half-hidden under the overhang's thickly matted chaparral. Here it was suddenly cooler, and the distant brawl of running water reached my ears. A rattlesnake coiled in the sun on a ledge twenty yards off the trail, ignoring the clatter of hooves. From the opposite slope a pair of buzzards flapped adrift and hovered drunkenly against the burnished cyanide blue of the sky.

For a mile or two the going was a little tricky, even at a walking pace, and there were moments when I'd have felt a lot safer in a jeep. The horses did not seem to agree. They were plainly enjoying themselves, and as much in a hurry to get

there as the track would allow. The water noise
approached more quickly, a sizable creek that
foamed through a series of spirited little rapids.
We splashed across without much difficulty, but
the stream failed to match the booming sound
that echoed down the gorge.

"There's a fall ahead," I said, turning around
in the saddle.

She smiled at me mischievously as if she'd got
the best of me in a game of hide-and-seek. She
nudged the sorrel forward, laid the riding crop
along its flank and recklessly charged up the trail
in a cloud of dust. She had vanished among the
rocks before I could kick Prince into chasing
after her. It took me five minutes to catch up,
and by then the falls were in sight, spurting from
lofty battlements, twin jets thundering down on
a granite shelf and leaping from there through
sun-slashed rainbow mists into the strangely
placid oval pond they had carved for themselves
in the canyon's bottom.

Here there were flowers again, verbena and
primrose and Spanish bayonet, terraced sweep-
ingly down to the edge of the pond. A dozen ancient sycamores wept into the limpid waters.
They cast harsh shadows over it that joined
together in an Oriental-temple silhouette. A lonely chipmunk scampered up the nearest tree at
our approach and twittered angrily at us about
the penalties for trespassing. The horses whin-
nied in their eagerness to get at the wild grapes
that covered the banks.

I unbuckled my saddlebags, packed tight with
our picnic lunch, and turned the horses loose.

The girl I had brought here to propose to stood expectantly watching me, childishly pleased. "Rick, isn't this marvelous?"

"You really want to know what I think?"

"Do I?" She parried the look in my eyes in a hurry and preoccupied herself with pulling off her boots and socks, and rolling up the legs of her jeans. "My feet are hot," she confessed in a very small voice, and ran like a yearling gazelle for the pond.

I pretended to ignore her and proceeded to lay out supplies on a caterer's napkin in a convenient shady spot. Joe Cornero had thought of everything in a hurry. But his sense of humor, if that was the word for it, appealed to me about as much as an open elevator shaft. There was a whole cold chicken, two paper containers of mixed *antipasto*, a dozen Italian bread sticks, a jug of Chianti and a double serving of *spumoni* ice cream carefully preserved in a Thermos pack. I gazed upon this elegant culinary array with my lips drawn back to here and the little hairs bristling down my neck until I remembered that this might be exactly his idea of a high-class alfresco repast. It was in either case too late to pick up the stitches. Lorna came racing back bare-legged through the flowers, excitedly waving a rock at me the size of a fist.

"Look what I found! The water's full of them, would you believe it?"

I looked, and took it away from her, and tossed it aside with a shrug.

"Mica ore. Fool's gold, they call it."

"Isn't that a shame?" She inspected the festive

board with casual approval. "You've picked all my favorite dishes, and I'm simply ravenous. . . ."

But the damage was done. Half an hour later, holding hands with her as we lay back among the scents of verbena and incienso grass, I felt a good deal less sure of myself. I wondered if by any chance I was about to throw away my aces on the draw. The jackass in me reasoned that I had, as it was, gone pretty far out on a limb. For all I knew, and in spite of Eve Garand's prompting, she might still consider the Hitchcock boy a valuable catch. She'd be twenty-one next month—Vanni's contemptuous dismissal of the fact twitched through my mind: *After that, chickie, you're on your own.* Even if she'd give me an edge on this wealthy though somewhat temperamental young swain, I'd have to offer her something a little more appetizing than outright squalor in return. The Big Fellow had perceived this clearly enough, and for that very purpose had provided the Bermuda bait, the ready-made glamour of an orchestra leader on the resort-hotel merry-go-round.

I decided I couldn't afford to tell her first and ask her later. It sounds calculating now, fairly nastily so, but actually what made me back out was the abrupt and devastating realization that I couldn't face the risk; that the mere thought of losing her was utterly unbearable.

"You're worrying again," she told me suddenly, matter-of-factly, as if there were nothing unusual about this disturbing faculty of hers that could probe my moods with almost telepathic accuracy.

"Just trying to figure out something."

"Can I help?"

"I don't know. I guess you could, if you wanted to. It's about a remark you made last night that's been bothering me ever since. You said that when people are in love there's never any doubt."

"You don't agree?"

"It's like saying that aspirins will cure a headache. I'm not a doctor, so I couldn't give you much of an argument on that, either, not without sounding off. I've always heard that the one essential element of love is doubt, a million different kinds of it. Doubt of yourself and doubt of each other. You're supposed to wonder if you can possibly, with all your faults and weaknesses, measure up to the occasion. You can't understand what the other sees in you, and you fully expect to prove yourself a bitter disappointment. You can't believe your own good fortune in ever having met someone who could be genuinely fond of you, and you're tempted to suspect an ulterior motive, or even a deliberate hoax. You feel sure there must be others who have a much better claim, staked out long ago. They tell me even people who've been married happily for many years still need to reassure each other all the time. But I don't know enough about it myself. You see, I've never been in love before."

Her hand in mine was very cool and small and tense. "You're being awfully serious now," she accused me in a tiny voice.

"Sorry. It sort of proves the point, though, doesn't it? Because it seems I can't make up my mind on how to handle this. There's doubt for you again. Not for a moment in the sense of questioning my love for you, but in feeling hopelessly confused about how to convince you. I made a mess of that last night and now I've lost the light touch altogether. I guess you'll have to help me after all.''

She drew back a little and sat up slowly, turning half around to look at me. It was a pose of such bewitching grace as to verge on the provocative, but the dark sapphires of her eyes were searching mine, solemnly inquisitive. ''Are you making this up as you go along?''

''You asked me what I was worrying about, and I told you. Maybe I made a mistake.''

''Do you love me, Rick?''

''You know I do.''

''Then say it.''

''I love you. Believe it or not. I haven't got the brains to say it any other way.''

''I wouldn't want to hear it any other way,'' she whispered, and with an adorable childish dignity of movement she suddenly leaned over me and found my lips.

You are the promised kiss of springtime. . . .

The falls were roaring in my ears and taking me down with them, fast and spinning dizzily through the rainbow mists, the heady fragrance of Shalimar: silk and velvet and the ardor of the desert sun itself. Tenderness, and the defiant flash of red carnation nails, arms like twin bands of steel, a timeless dark of tears and strangest rapture—*all the things you are*—until at last she cried out my name, a high-pitched cry of ecstasy and sweet despair. Then after a while there was light again, and the temple of the sycamores around us, the flowers and the rushing waters and our horses browsing among the wild grapes on the bank.

Time passed us by while words had lost their meaning. The sun's decline below the canyon's ramparts brought a sudden chill and broke the spell.

"I've got to know . . . ."

"What, Rick?"

"When it happened. What made you decide. I'm an idiot to ask you, because I haven't the faintest idea myself."

"I don't, either. Cross my heart. Not when it *happened*. But I've a horrible confession to make. It was I who talked Eve into coming over to your table in the card room Tuesday night, when you were playing that silly game all by yourself. See what a brazen wench I am?"

"I see. That's just too bad. Now you'll have to make an honest man of me."

She drew herself up with mock severity. "Such gallantry, Sir Knight!"

"I mean it. You can't expect to toy with my affections like this and get away with it."

"I should hope not. Are you by any chance proposing?"

"Yes, ma'am, I am.."

"Go right ahead. I'll listen carefully."

"Sweet lady, will you marry me?"

"Yes, Rick. Yes, yes, yes. Anytime, anywhere. If you really want me to." Once more the canyon walls reeled crazily.

"Tonight?"

"Yes, darling, tonight. Do you think we can?"

"It's only a hundred and fifty miles to Yuma, Arizona. They give you service round the clock."

"Then we won't need to drive so fast. I don't want anything to happen now. Not until we get there." She picked up her hat and shook out her glossy black locks and smiled at me. The smile was both gay and serene, and it shook me to the marrow. I fished my pockets for a cigarette with trembling hands and thought, this is it, last call for purgatory. Play it straight, or in a day or two you'll be stepping off a chair with your belt around your neck. But somehow the target kept eluding me, so finally I got off a deflection shot.

"You want to know what really had me worried?"

"Oh, I can guess. It was Eve's needling you behind my back." She looked as mischievous as a small kitten with a ball of yarn. "I put her up to it. Wasn't that mean of me?"

"You didn't put her up to telling me about a lad with a big foreign car," I said.

She would have giggled if she'd been the giggling type, but my ears caught a certain overtone.

"Not Stu Hitchcock! He's just a little boy...."

"The way I heard, you were engaged to him."

"I was not!" The dark blue eyes were bright with indignation. "He's spread that story over town, and all I ever did was go out on a date with him once or twice, and then only because he twisted my arm. Rick, have you ever met him?"

"You could call it that, I suppose."

"Well, then, you must know. He's so spoiled

and conceited and possessive and altogether insufferable, and still he'll make a pass at anything in skirts, on sight. I couldn't even help feeling sorry for him at first. So I tried to be nice to him, in a sisterly way, and the next thing I knew there were two of those gushing society editors on the phone, asking me to confirm that we were about to elope! I got rid of them somehow and I called Stu, and when he came over I almost had to hit him before he would behave.''

"And you went on from there letting him take you for a ride," I said.

"Yes, two days later he dropped by, just when I'd got this job at the hotel, and he sort of apologized and promised not to see me again for two weeks. So I told him he could drive me out if he'd be sure to keep his hands to himself. Anyway, I can manage him," she wound up naively.

"Uh-huh. With a baseball bat, you can."

Now she was laughing at me. "It doesn't really matter, darling, does it? Not anymore. Because I'm eloping with you, not with Stu Hitchcock. And the reason is *not* that I've always wanted a honeymoon in Bermuda."

"Does it have to be Bermuda?" I mumbled, biting my lip. But she didn't even hear me; she was intent upon her pocket mirror, studying her face from a dozen different angles, like an art critic confronted by something in the neoclassicist school.

"I think I got burned," she said composedly. "That stuff I put on isn't any use. Rick, it's getting dark; we'll have to hurry to be back in time for dinner."

I climbed to my feet and started packing up the picnic remains. "There's still a lot I want to talk to you about."

"We'll have a lot of time," she reminded me fondly, and stood on tiptoe to kiss the lobe of my left ear. "Will you play for me every night, pretty music like yesterday's?"

"Sure, every night."

"You're not worried again, are you, darling? About... little things, formalities? We can wait a few days, if there's any trouble with the regulations or anything like that."

"There won't be. Arizona doesn't bother with blood tests, or a waiting period. They don't even care about parents' consent if you tell them you're over eighteen."

She snuggled an arm under mine and smiled seraphically up into my eyes.

"I'm over eighteen, darling," she confided. "And I have no parents or family of any kind in the whole wide world...."

14

THE RHYTHM OF THE FALLS continued to drum
through my head for most of the homebound
ride, without ever succeeding in shutting out the
cruel echo of her words. Dusk on the narrow
mountain trail made further conversation easy to
avoid; my silence did not become embarrassing
until we were cantering side by side across the
valley of the desert again, with our horses snort-
ing eagerly for the stable. This time she made little effort to draw me out. Once she mentioned,
"I thought you wanted to talk. . ." and gave me
a puzzled glance when my only reaction was a
frown. Later, with the cluster of lights from the
Hacienda del Sol spaced out before us under a
slowly rising moon, she shyly reached to pat the
pinto's straining neck.

"I must call Mr. Biedermayer right away."

"What for?"

"The advertising pictures, silly. He'll have to
find another girl to pose for him."

It was an interesting point, and one that had
not quite occurred to me before. I let it drift
downstream; there did not seem much sense in
arguing about it now. The date-palm orchards
were already closing in around us, and a bow-

legged stable hand was waiting for us at the corral gate, smirking up the sleeves of his tattered blue denims. My watch was still out of commission, but he told me it was seven o'clock. We'd made it back in time for dinner after all.

Our walk through the park amounted to something of an ordeal, in one of those bellowing silences peculiar to lovers in distress. On the porch steps of her bungalow she finally, half-heartedly, confronted me with it, anxiously watching me from the shadows, looking very small and frightened and submissive. "Rick, what's wrong?"

"Nothing's wrong. I'm tired, that's all."

"Are you sure? Have I done something you— misunderstood?"

"No," I said flatly. "No. It would have been completely impossible to misunderstand you."

She touched my arm timidly as if to reassure herself that it was I. "You sound so strange, my love," she told me, struggling hard for gaiety. "You'd almost have me believe that you rather regret what happened. Do you?"

"No, of course I don't."

"Want me to dress up and make myself look pretty for you?"

"That would be nice," I said, taking pains to suppress the croak in my voice. "You might give me a buzz when you're ready. Don't start packing yet. We can do that after we eat."

"All right." She clung to me, her arms around my neck. "Tell me again, Rick. Please!"

"I love you. Very much."

She sighed contentedly and brushed my lips and lightly ran up the steps.

In my own quarters I sat on the bed for a while, smoking and brooding and still wearing Joe Cornero's Stetson and his fancy high-heeled boots. The full-length mirror on the wardrobe door informed me that they suited me just fine. I was doing pretty well for myself with other people's property, and no mistake. Maybe I should apply for a patent and go into business.

I pitched the hat into a corner, as if that would do any good, and jerked off the boots and stalked into the bathroom, turning the shower on full strength. I was still punishing myself with a towel when the knocking started.

The knocking was rapid, persistent and urgent, and much too furtive for a maid on a mission to turn down the sheets, or a bellhop with a message. It was the kind of knocking that sounds worse than a scream in the night, the kind that only country doctors are likely to hear more than once in a lifetime. It froze me to the spot before I could so much as catch my breath. Then I used up some of that to swear, and the rest for racing like a maniac across the apartment to the door.

There was blood on her hands. Not a lot of it, but the smears were fresh and scarlet bright. She was still in her riding togs, and holding herself erect with an almost casual gracefulness, as if she'd merely called to borrow a cake of soap. Her complexion was a dull, shadow-flecked ivory.

"Could you come to my place for a moment?" she asked me in well-bred, carefully modulated tones, like a little girl reciting on daddy's birthday. She did not even see me, or the towel around my loins.

"Are you hurt?"

"Oh, no. I'm perfectly all right, thank you."

"Wait inside. Close the door," I snapped, and dashed back into the bedroom for my clothes. Dressing must have taken me all of thirty seconds, with the knowledge of impending disaster clawing at my nerves. When I returned she was exactly where I'd left her, still standing up straight on the porch, one bloodstained hand half lifted to the very point where her knock had been answered by me. I shuddered and slapped her face, twice, and not gently.

"Snap out of it, will you!"

She blinked back the tears that wanted to flow, and her shoulders sagged into sudden dejection, but the razor edge of hysteria had been blunted. "Please, Rick, come quickly. I need your help...."

It was twenty yards to the bungalow next door. She'd left the lights on in the living room, the front door ajar. I covered the distance in five or six bounds, gained the porch in one jump and stopped short in my tracks on the threshold.

The room was not badly disturbed. It was the same impersonally cheerful copy of my own that had somehow upset and excited me on my visit the afternoon before. There was still *Harper's Bazaar* on the coffee table, and the bottle-green leather purse and gloves on the couch. The carpet had been scuffed a little here and there, and a chair overturned as if by accident, and the long, ornamental brass poker from the French provincial fireplace stand had been dropped in the middle of the floor.

On the edge of the heavy green nylon rug, near the Mexican archway to the bedroom, slumped the body of Stuart Hitchcock.

He was lying on his back, legs scissored out, trunk askew at an unnatural angle in its jacket of crumpled blue suede. His arrogant young head wasn't blond anymore. I had seen heads like that before, by the dozen, and I wasn't much impressed by the remnants of the dainty little first-aid kit with which she'd tried to fix up the deal. I snatched for his pulse and couldn't find any; his shirt popped a couple of buttons while my fingers groped for a heartbeat. The skin felt hot and dry, and between the ribs I caught a slight, irregular flutter.

"Is it . . . bad?"

She'd come in after me and stood beside me, watching helplessly. I got up and glanced at the phone in the bedroom and said grimly, "Six miles to the nearest hospital. He'll never make it, but we'll have to try. If he forced you to hit him, why couldn't you have used that gadget over there?"

Her flashy little silver-plated riding crop was on the copy of *Harper's Bazaar*. It couldn't have done any real damage, but its blow would have served to discourage the attentions of a drunken longshoreman. She looked at it, and at me, and at the poker on the carpet, and said, "Oh!" blankly, as if I'd just explained about the bomb.

Stu Hitchcock stirred an arm and produced a grating noise in his throat. His pale bloodshot eyes were suddenly open and staring at her with

a waspish malignancy. It was the kind of stare
that will focus on a pinpoint and observe almost
nothing else; I am convinced he was never aware
of my presence in the room. He licked his lips and
spoke up clearly in surprisingly loud, vigorous
tones. "You..." he said, and added a single
word, the one he had flung in my face five days
earlier when my car got in his way. Before I had a
chance to stop him he managed to lift himself a
few inches on one elbow until the rug slipped
under him. His head struck the hardwood floor
with a soggy thump. This time I tore the shirt in
my haste to check on his heart. The flutter had
disappeared.

"That pocket mirror of yours," I said dully.
"Give it to me."

She nearly dropped it. She was trembling all
over now and crying quietly, hiding behind a
wad of Kleenex. I pushed her into a chair and
tried the mirror, a small plain disk of stainless
steel. It refused to cloud, and the bleeding had
slowed to a trickle.

"How did he get in?"

She did not hear me and I had to shout. Then
she could only mumble at me, about maybe forgetting to lock up that morning. It didn't make
much difference; he could have got a passkey for
the asking. I started to pace the room, wrestling
with the ghastly mess she was in. I didn't even
stop to consider my own position, simply because
that would have complicated things to a point
where I'd need a slide rule and a carload of blue-
prints.

The cops were out, I knew that much. Under

different circumstances she might have come out
on top, on a plea of self-defense, or at worst
they'd have put her in storage for a year or two
and tipped the parole board to leave the key in
the mailbox. As it was, with her background and
everything, she'd be lucky to draw five to ten,
and luckier still if she made it to the penitentiary
alive. No two ways about it, her only chance was
to pass the dice, to me. Remove Stu's body, take
it through the back door to my place, clean up
hers and exchange pokers. I could make a run for
it, draw all suspicion away from her. I knew the
ropes and I'd move quickly; if they caught me in
the end it wouldn't matter a lot, not anymore. I
didn't get much of a kick from the idea, or any
romantic notions about knight-errantry. It just
seemed as if I owed her that much, to make up
for what I'd let myself be talked into doing to
her, regardless of whether she was good, bad or
indifferent.

I'd have to have money, though, and plenty of
it. Without money I couldn't gain time, and time
was the essence of the deal—time for the dust to
settle, and for her to collect her wits, and for
everybody's memory to grow a little shorter, a
little less alert. As long as I could keep them chasing after me, time would be running in our favor.
I glanced at the electric clock over the
mantelpiece; it startled me to see the hands still
short of seven-thirty. There was a slip of paper
on the marble shelf under the clock. It looked
like a message from the front desk that had been
pushed under the door, picked up, read and put
aside there. I looked at it myself and dropped it

in her lap. "Miss Ryan: Mr. Vanni phoned at 9:45, 10:30 and 11:00 A.M. He wants you to return his calls as soon as you come in."

"What are you waiting for?" I asked her carefully.

She stared at the message between sobs, as if she had never seen it before.

"Go on, call him back," I said. "Get him to hurry over right away, alone. Tell him to bring ten grand, to take care of a real emergency. I'm picking up the check for you, and I'll need the bread to keep moving."

She instantly caught the play; it woke her up like a shot in the arm. She was out of her chair and had a double handful of my coat before I'd finished. The hysterics were over—she knew I wouldn't stop for anything but sober, air-conditioned reason.

"Rick, you can't! I won't let you do it. I won't, do you hear?"

"You'll have no choice. Not the way I'm stacking the cards. If you throw in your hand after that we'll both of us be crucified."

She began to push me to the door. "You've got to get out of here. Please, darling. I'm going to call the police."

It was quite a switch, and the joke was on me. I had to lay it on the line but fast, shock her into accepting the situation. "Know who he is?" I pressed her, pointing with my chin.

"Of course I do. Rick, listen to me—"

"No, you don't. He's the only son of the biggest crime-syndicate boss west of Chicago, and you've just booked yourself a nice cold drawer in the county morgue. I happen to know it because I was hired by him five days ago to slam the lid on your sisterly affections for his precious boy. You see, he doesn't approve of you at all, and he figures it might be a little expensive to buy you off the track.''

She kept clinging to me. She'd buried her face in my shoulder and I couldn't make out if she was crying or laughing. "Sure it's funny," I said. "All of it is. The way I've fallen for you like a ton of bricks, and we were going to be married tonight and live happily ever after, just like in the story books. We'd have made such a charming couple, you and I—the fancy lady of a rich Italian roué, and a penniless, neurotic stooge for the mob. Now will you be sensible and get on that phone, or do I have to call the guy myself?''

She let go of my coat and looked up at me. It was a curiously steady gaze, unclouded by emotion—searching, perhaps, but surely unafraid. The tears had gone and left few traces of their passage. She appeared to me more beautiful, and more heartbreakingly desirable, in those brief moments than she ever had before. As it is, I shall probably never find out what she intended to do. Time had run out for us; the fates had kept their final irony in store. I did not even hear the front-door lock snap back, but the sudden cold draft from the evening breeze swept my neck and twisted me around.

Steve Kovacs carried a black canvas satchel, the kind some of the more old-fashioned banks still get their payroll messengers to use. He put it down, and pushed his hat back for an inch or two on his shinily pomaded elderly gigolo curls, and buried his hands in the bulky slash pockets of his stylish brown camel's-hair coat. The gesture conveyed no particular menace. He was plainly amused with me and prepared to make allowances.

"Hello, piahno player," he said, and the sneer he supplied me was almost indulgent.

15

THEY CAME TROOPING IN behind him through the door in a grim sort of conga line, stepping on each other's heels and hunching their shoulders as if they were already bringing in the coffin. I wasn't even very much surprised to see them, and none of them paid much attention to me. The market in stooges had collapsed around my ears.

The Big Fellow himself pushed past me without seeming to notice any of us at all. He stood squarely on the edge of the rug, thumbing his bushy gray field marshal's mustache and dispassionately watching Kovacs, who had squatted by the body of his son to examine it with the swift dexterity of a trained ambulance intern. It confused me that none of them gave evidence of being shocked; apparently they had arrived expecting nothing less than what was there for them to find. Max Gonzalez, the Tahquitz Casino handyman, was resting his back against the doorpost and smiling absentmindedly; his long, swarthy, handsome-gorilla mug looked vaguely pleased, and when I caught his eye he actually winked at me. The Irish pug with the groggy bass had hooked a leg over one corner of the couch and displayed an air of stolid boredom. His chauf-

feur's uniform was dusty, and the black whip-
cord cap he wore at a jaunty angle had its visor
dented and a three-inch tear in the crown.

Of the whole bunch, only Alfredo Vanni
showed any signs of being ill at ease. He looked
smaller and chunkier still, and all his Thespian
self-assurance had been drained from him. The
only gestures he was permitting himself had to
do with mopping up the rush of sweat across his
olive brow. He kept staring at the poker at his
feet, as if the damned thing had managed to
fascinate him beyond measure; he never once so
much as glanced at Lorna or at me. I couldn't
think what he was doing there. His arrival with
the others made about as much sense as bringing
Figaro on stage in the last act of *Götterdäm-
merung*.

It didn't take me long to find out all about it.
Steve Kovacs got up, brushed the lint off his
knees and shrugged. He saw the message on the
floor and snatched it off the carpet like a hawk
diving on a pigeon. I felt suddenly a little dizzy
taking in the pitch, dizzy with incredulous relief
and quick bewilderment. They suspected the
Italian, not the girl! Somehow they had known
this would happen, and they'd come all the way
from the city to pick up the pieces. It occurred to
me then that Lorna had never admitted to striking the boy. She might have come in and found
him there, and wasted ten minutes or so in trying
to patch him up with her silly little bandages and
vials of antiseptic, before she'd become panicky
and run to me for help.

And I'd stopped her from calling the cops. . . .

We needed them now, worse than we needed food and water for the next six months. We needed a yacht, and a million dollars, a trip to the moon, and a company of United States Marines. We needed to live for another half an hour.

The Big Fellow was reading the message and scowling at it. He seemed to be keeping his temper nicely under wraps. I didn't like that, and I didn't like the dull red flush below his tan, or the throbbing little veins in his temples. The harsh rust brown eyes had a glassy squint in them that did not look quite sane. Even Max dropped his meaningless smirk in a hurry when he saw it. Steve Kovacs sneered at Vanni and spoke the first words to be uttered by any of us since they'd walked in.

"You want I should get the sheriff already, Meester Hitchcock?" he inquired, rather flatly and without a hint of scorn, surprising me almost as much as if he had offered to buy me a drink.

The voice from the gravel pit cleared itself and said brusquely, "Not yet. Make him write it down first and sign it. We got to have proof."

Kovacs nodded and turned to the little walnut desk behind the couch. He pulled out a drawer, produced some sheets of stationery and a pen. These he laid out ceremoniously on the blotter, turned to Vanni and bowed from the waist, his haggard, deeply grooved features suave like those of a nightclub maître d'hôtel. The effect was something right out of a nightmare, the spoiled-lobster kind where you wake up yelling off your head.

Fat little Figaro kept mopping up the sweat and

studying the poker at his toes. He did not look
the least bit romantic anymore. "Whatsamatta
you want me to write?" he protested. "Is big
mistake you fellows make. I no kill 'im, I tell you.
Wanna talk to Mees Ryan, door open, she not in.
Find these fellow on floor, don't know 'im, never
see 'im before. Santa Maria, whatta you think,
eh? You think Vanni go around killing people,
they never been introduced?"

He got no laughs or anything; we were probably the toughest house he'd ever played. I was
watching Lorna cling intensely to my arm and
stare at him with wide, shocked, disbelieving
eyes. *Such gallantry, Sir Knight. . . .* Kovacs just
sneered and asked him, "Why you run away?"

"Sure, okay, so I run. Is bad business, eh, bad
publicity, Vanni get caught on a spot, whatta you
expect? Means reporters, photographers, people
from studio, alla time jump up and down, break-a
contract maybe, no damn good. These fellow on
floor, he is dead, you understand. I no can 'elp.
What you do in my place, eh? Maybe you stick
around and raise-a big fuss?"

Walter Hitchcock cleared his throat again, not
too successfully. "The confession, Steve," he
rasped. "Get him to write it down."

"I no write anything. Make-a confess, go to jail
maybe, whatsamatta you fellows, I'm crazy?"

The little Irish chauffeur swung one dangling
foot and kicked him squarely in the tail. For just
a kick it had plenty of judgment, style and ex-
perience. It lifted a couple of hundred pounds
clean off the rug and sent it staggering across the
room, into the chair that Kovacs held obligingly

behind the desk. Its sudden, coarse brutality brought the hackles away from my neck, as much as I'd seen it coming. Someone said loudly in a tight, urgent voice, "Go on, you chump, what are you waiting for? Don't you know when you're getting the breaks?" There was a second or two of silence before I realized the voice had been my own.

He heard me all right. He picked up the pen and jerked himself around in the chair. It must have been the first time he recognized me, and the surprise of it was almost low comedy, a perfect, horrified double take that shook him to the core. He threw up his hands, saw Lorna beside me and shouted at her raucously in something pretty close to despair, "You know this man?"

Her fingers bit into my arm; the red carnation nails actually cut through the sleeve to my skin. "Yes, Alfred, I know him," she told him steadily. "We're going to be married," she added, just as calmly as if this was just another cocktail party for her birthday.

"But these man, he is a gambler, a dirty crook! He came to my 'ouse last night, you understand, makes like big-shot publicity man, ask many questions about you, act very strange. I check with studio, they never heard of him, call me back all excited—is very bad character, these man! So I call you all day, I come myself at last, alla time you are out. Now you tell me you marry the guy!"

"I love him," she said, hardly moving her lips. "I'm sorry, Alfred."

He threw up his arms again in a gesture of helpless perplexity and turned his back on us. For a moment he hunched at the desk, pen in hand, then spoke to her again over his shoulder. "You want me to write-a confess?" He sounded puzzled and hurt, like a very small boy who was about to be sent to bed without supper for something he didn't do.

She glanced up at me and saw my hasty nod. "Perhaps you should," she said coolly. "Do what you think best. The police will take care of things as soon as they get here."

He threw the pen away and swept blotter and letterheads off the desk in one vicious burst of defiance. "I no kill these fellow!" he screamed. "No make-a confess! Go ahead, call-a cops, is okay, I call myself!" He had lapsed into an almost inarticulate jabbering. He lurched for the bedroom archway and fell flat on his face when Steve Kovacs slid out a leg and neatly tripped him up.

The Big Fellow stepped out of his way and frowned at all of us impartially. "Make him quit stalling," he ordered. It was a growl that cut straight to the bone.

The little Irishman got off the couch and came over, hitching up his breeches. He shot a doubtful glance over his shoulder at the window blinds.

"There's the customers, chief. They won't like the noise," he said conversationally, and reached for Vanni's collar.

"Then get him out of here."

All at once everybody got busy, as if court had been adjourned and it was time to go to lunch.

Hitchcock himself turned on his heels and stalked out through the back door without wasting another scowl on the body of his son. Kovacs grabbed up a handful of stationery and ran after him. The Irish chauffeur had yanked Vanni's jacket halfway down his spine and was hustling him off in their wake as easily as if he were coaxing a child. Max Gonzalez unbuttoned his loose-fitting black raglan and produced from its inner recesses a long-barreled Mauser pistol. He came up with an old-fashioned carbine stock of vulcanized rubber and a forty-shot spiral magazine, clipped the whole piece together in two brisk movements that made a single click, and cradled it lightly across his left arm.

"Let's get on the ball, Bailey," he said, winking at me.

I looked at the gun without much curiosity. Guns had been shown to me before, in a lot of different sizes and shapes. I had cared for them, fed them, slept with them for two long years. I'd been hit by them twice and missed by them so many times I couldn't have kept track of it with a computer. This was kind of a nice-looking gun. It would need regular oiling and stripping and exercising, and Max was just the boy who would see to such things, the way a master mechanic takes pride in his tools. A long-barreled Mauser on a stock is lighter, handier, more accurate and only a shade less in a hurry than your common or kitchen variety of bullet sprinkler. It is not just another hunk of hardware to start an argument with. I took my shoulders off the wall reluctantly and said, "Leave the lady out of this, huh, Max?"

"Aw, now, you know me, Bailey. I got nothing but respect for the ladies. I always figure suppose they was my mother or my sister, see what I mean?" He grinned at me winningly and waved the Mauser at the open door. "Let's all of us tag along and watch the fun, whaddayasay?"

"No, Max, let's not," I said. "Miss Ryan stays right here."

He didn't drop his grin, but the gun swung around and peered at my liver as if it were interested in examining the color of same. Lorna caught her breath sharply and said, "Rick..." like a prayer, and tugged at my arm with all her weight. I shrugged and gave up. Crowding Max was pointless, of course. The next voice we wouldn't even hear would be the coroner's.

Outside the evening breeze was already dying, and the moon was big and bright as a new silver dollar. The desert looked bleak and cold, and incredibly lonely in spite of the vast and swelling chorus of the crickets, the cloying aroma of sagebrush and jasmine. The others were already halfway down the sandy lane that led into the massive darkness of the date-palm grove. Max motioned us along and strolled a few feet behind us, snapping a match to life on his free thumb to light a cigarette.

"Me, I don't go so much for that wop," he observed companionably. "They tell me he sings pretty good, but he don't have no class. Look at it this way, Mr. Bailey—say me and you was to waste a guy, and we was to be caught with our pants down taking a powder, we wouldn't put up no stalls. We'd say, gee whiz, why, sure we done it, you guys wanna make something of it, go ahead. Now the wop, he ain't even satisfied to get the breaks, like you said, on account of he don't like the publicity, how about that!''

"Why bother about a confession?" I asked. "It'll never stand up in court."

"Aw, now, Mr. Bailey—you kidding? He wastes Mr. Stuart, don't he, and we come in, and we arrest him, see, all nice and legal, and he confesses, and then while we're calling the sheriff he gets away from us in his car. So we chase him in ours, and we throw a couple slugs at his tires, and he just happens to be fresh outta luck. Him being in the movies and all, you know how it is, we got to take a little trouble. Like for instance coming up with a real confession where he lays it on the line, in his own writing, the D.A.'s got experts, they can check it for themselves. . . .''

The girl who was still clinging to my arm made a faint little whimper and missed her step. I steadied her quickly and touched her hand, trying to pretend reassurance. They were going to work it all right. It would be a brazen stunt, but they'd get by with it. In California any citizen can make an arrest on the scene of a crime, and the law allows him to use all reasonable force in preventing or halting the escape of his prisoner.

The only catch to it in this case was easy to remove. It consisted of two people who were not in the movies, who would cause very little trouble and who had been fresh out of luck for quite some time. They were the only witnesses who'd be in a position to talk out of turn, and by a strange coincidence their names were Lorna Ryan and Richard Bailey.

We were entering the date-palm grove behind the others, and it wasn't dark there after all, not nearly dark enough. Still, the trees made for cover—a sudden dash into the underbrush would have offered me a chance. To a tired, hysterical girl in boots and riding clothes it offered none at all. Max Gonzalez did not seem to worry about it. His mood continued both affable and garrulous. "The wop's got it coming to him," he told me with much of the good-natured contempt of one Latin for another. "Wanna hear something funny, Mr. Bailey? He asked for it himself!"

"Oh, go on with you, Max," I said absently. "I suppose he called the Big Fellow and told him to come on down, he'd just laid out his son with a poker!"

"Well, gee whiz, how'd you know?" he demanded, playing surprised. "Yeah, he called us all right, bright 'n' early this morning. Seems he got in a jam with a couple of shills from this poker store down in Formosa the boss has been wiring for sound since they opened six weeks ago. They take the wop for a hundred and eighty grand at gin last night. He finally rumbles the play, so they cool him with the tear-up gag and clear out fast. Some pal of his tips their mitt when they're gone, and the wop puts in a squawk to us, we should give him service on the deal, see what I mean?"

I saw what he meant: I was the pal who'd said a fond goodbye at 3:00 A.M. and mentioned in passing that one check looks just like another, you can't always tell which is which when it comes to tearing them up. He'd laughed at me then, but he wasn't laughing anymore. "What happened?" I asked Max, pretending to humor him.

"Keep walking, Mr. Bailey. The boss gives him service, like he wants—we protect our clients, see, or we don't stay in business. Me and Steve and Mike, we pick up these characters the minute they leave the bank this morning. We shake 'em up a bit, and run 'em over to Formosa, and Mike busts up the joint but real good. Then the boss, he figures on how this wop has got connections, it'd be worth it to return the dough to him in person, so we get on rolling to Palm Springs. We're just outside Pomona when Mr. Stuart goes by in the English buggy of his heading east like a bat outta hell, and right away the boss starts worrying and says he'll lay us nine to five that Mr. Stuart's come down with a case of big ears, he must've overheard some crack Steve made to us about the wop and this young lady here. . . ."

We'd emerged from the grove and passed the tennis courts and arrived at the pool, where the rest of our party clustered on the cool blue tiles in front of the cabana. The pool lay quietly shimmering in the moonlight, its surface barely ruffled by the dying breeze still whispering in through the tangerine bower. The wind had tossed in a few drifting hibiscus blooms, and among them a handful of desert bugs were helplessly paddling around in circles. It made a charming spot for signing a confession, and it offered by all means sufficient privacy to keep the customers from complaining about the noise.

"So that's what made you decide to pay us a visit," I said to Max, not because I wanted confirmation, but simply for the sake of what little relief could be had from listening to myself.

"Yeah, if Mike could've stepped on it we might've made it in time to spoil the show," he told me cheerfully. "But the boss don't like to drive fast, and I guess he didn't figure on this much of a score. Mr. Stuart must have gained half an hour on us for the trip. We was just pulling in to park when the wop, he comes hot-footing it into the lot for his car, and of course we latch onto him quick, and he gives us this spiel about how he walks in and there's a dead guy on the floor he never seen before. How corny can you get, huh, Mr. Bailey?"

The unfortunate subject of this instructive disquisition seemed to have regained a certain amount of his dignity. Mike, the chauffeur, had released his collar, and now he could use his arms again to talk. He was still visibly in nothing like a mood to oblige with a little scribbling job—such as, for instance, his own death sentence. They were still trying to jockey him into it; they didn't like to mess him up too much for the autopsy people to get ideas. Mike was taking it easy, standing by and stoking up his pipe with one of those trick pocket lighters that will jet down the flame into the bowl, like a miniature blowtorch. Steve Kovacs looked up at our little procession and jerked a thumb.

"Inside," he snapped, and added nastily, "Iss very nice, we got piahno player. Make pretty music for us yet, piahno player!"

I could feel Lorna shivering against my arm, and the ice cubes forming in my stomach. "Now wait a minute . . . " I protested queasily before he cut me short with a venomous glare.

"Make pretty music. *Basta*."

Max Gonzalez jabbed the muzzle of the Mauser into me persuasively enough to make me wince. "Just relax, Mr. Bailey, will ya, please?" he suggested, and herded us along into the bathhouse.

There was plenty of light in there. The big patio door had been left wide open and the Blüthner's gaudy nightclub coat of burnished nacre glittered eerily under the moon. Lorna sank into a chair and buried her face in the cushions. Max rested his shoulder on the casement frame and waved me to the bench. He looked all of ten feet tall; the crown of his hat touched the roof. "You heard," he said crisply. "Start tickling them ivories."

"What for?" I demanded. "Now listen, fun is fun, but this is plain screwy. You know I can't play with a gun in my ribs while you boys put that poor guy down there through the hoop. Nobody could."

"Sure you can, Mr. Bailey. Wanna make out you got no class? Be something to do with your hands while I'm keeping an eye on things."

That was it—he wanted to see the feature and not be bothered about my getting out of line. I shrugged and sat down on the bench, and ran through a couple of scales on two jittery fingers. From the bathhouse we had a ringside view all right, a few feet up and twenty yards away, too far to catch the sound track, but a lot too close to the screen for comfort: twenty miles too close. They were getting impatient with him, and they couldn't afford to waste all night or allow him to feel he was holding any cards. I saw Mike knock out his pipe on the tiles and put it away, saw

Kovacs drift out of the group and pick up the
hose that lay coiled around a hydrant for clean-
ing the deck. It was just that simple. One instant
little Figaro was still volubly arguing and
gesticulating, with his back to the diving board,
and the next he lay struggling in the water, struggling with a forty-pound pressure squirt from the
hose in his face.

Max Gonzalez chuckled and spoke to me over
his shoulder, tersely critical. "Let's have a
tune."

"You can hear this, can't you?"

"Yeah, I can hear this, and it stinks."

I grimaced and with a crash struck up Ravel's
Bolero, which would be about his speed by way
of a tune. The effect was macabre enough to set
the original Frankenstein monster on its ears, but
Max just nodded and turned back to watch
the big attraction. I set my teeth and measured
the distance while my hands kept hammering the
keys. It wasn't any use, he could drill his initials
through me before I could get up off the bench
and halfway across the room. Down at the pool
they weren't fooling anymore. They'd let Figaro
bob up to get his breath, and they'd yell at him
and wave a sheet of paper, and he'd shake a fist
at them and get the hose in his face again. The
way it sounds is like a joke, or a spot of summer-
camp horseplay, but he must have realized by
then why they wanted his signature so badly,
and of course that could only result in making
him hold out to the end. He didn't even know
enough to duck under the surface and try to
swim for it. He probably had pools of his own in

Malibu and in Beverly Hills besides the one at his place in Palm Springs, but all he could do was paddle in a circle with the bugs and fight to keep afloat.

I didn't wonder for a moment why his stubbornness should fail to puzzle them, or make them doubt his guilt. It never would occur to them that Stu could have been killed in anything except a row about the girl, and one in which she'd probably not even been present at that. The telephone message supplied her with an alibi of sorts; it made them believe she'd only just come in. In any case, they'd never have conceived a notion that she might herself have struck the blow. They were reasonable men who wouldn't think of killing even a fly without a good and sufficient motive. That let her out, and me, as well. I was only a stooge, after all, and stooges don't kill, they're hired for laughs.

And that left poor little Figaro, who'd come only to warn her, warn her about me and my funny-peculiar questions. The door had been open; he must have arrived while she'd run off to me for help. He hadn't realized that Stu was still alive, hadn't noticed the first-aid stuff she'd been trying to use on the boy. Just she and I knew these things, and she clearly intended to keep it that way. Somehow it shocked me that she'd let him pay the bill, though I had to admit to myself that they wouldn't have listened to her. And as it was, we'd all of us been carefully tagged for the undertaker from the minute they walked in on us.

My hands kept hammering out Ravel's jerky

rhythms, and my eyes kept flipping back and forth between the gun butt under Max Gonzalez's arm and the grisly, pathetic little scene at the pool. They were getting pretty cross down there—they'd been looking for a quick return on their money, and it wasn't coming off that way. Steve was playing the hose some more, and this time his victim did not come up for air when he shifted the stream. They stood around watching for a while, and then Mike made a sprint for the toolhouse and brought back a long-handled rake. He dragged it through the water from the end of the diving board and brought up the body, guiding it along and bracing himself to hoist it out on the tiles. He went through all this with the sober disdain of a workman performing his chores for the day. If you paid him his wages he'd drive your car, or plant your petunias, or skin you an elephant exactly like that.

Steve had turned off the hydrant and checked the deal. I didn't need his sneer, or the way he tapped his heart. It was all over: no more Figaro or Pagliacci or Rigoletto, no more flashing smiles and pretty girls and a million two for a couple of songs in the movies. No Duesenberg convertibles with horns that would play "O Sole Mio," no chemmy or dice or roulette, or gin at fifty bucks a point. Not anymore. There was nothing left now but a clumsy, waterlogged bundle of rags and cold meat. My fingers went stiff and slipped off the keyboard of their own accord.

The Mauser quickly swung around to look at me, and Max said, "Nuh-unh!" cozily as if he'd caught me reaching for the jam behind his back. I shrugged at him again and struck up the *Bolero* again, and just then they shouted to him to send down Lorna. That was when I almost rushed him regardless, and he appeared honestly surprised at the snarl on my face.

"What's with you, Mr. Bailey? Who spiked your Ovaltine?"

"Leave her alone. I'll talk to them."

"Sure you will," he promised me cheerfully. "You and her both, you'll be doing the talking. You seen the whole thing, when the wop takes a swing with this poker at Mr. Stuart, and we come in, and he lams outta there. So we all chase after him, and he does a flop into that pool and his ticker gives out. Ain't that how it was?"

He sounded casual enough to make my hair stand on end. The girl was already walking slowly down the ramp to where they were waiting for her, and I said hurriedly, "Yeah, that's how it was, all right," very loud. She gave no sign of having understood. She walked without pausing for an instant, gracefully, her head held high, her back quite straight, and slim to the verge of fragility. Steve Kovacs was holding a chair for her with a gaily striped sponge rubber pad, and on the glass-topped patio table he'd laid out his writing supplies. They were apparently determined to get something down in black and white. Mike seemed to be fiddling with his pipe again. The Big Fellow himself stood aside and was scowling on her without much interest.

Max turned to watch and said over his shoulder, "Let's have a tune!"

I swore at him under my breath and slapped

both hands back on the keys. My knee struck a shelf below the board and reminded me about the electrical player attachment. I stole a peek, and the blood started pounding at me from inside like a man with a hammer who wanted out. The "Poet and Peasant" overture was still in place, all set to roll.

They were cracking the whip at her down there. I could see Steve's expression and the motion of his arm, like a hatchet on kindling wood—make pretty music, *basta*! They had no more time to waste on arguments and she kept on shaking her head and refusing the pen he held out to her. I dropped Ravel and started improvising fast. It was a question of getting from a Spanish caprice in F to this piece of noisy German corn in D major, without the transition offending Max's suspicious ear. I made it at last, and flicked the switch on the keyboard at the top of a swift arpeggio. The motor picked up with a sudden whine, and the roll jerked ahead, the Blüthner's keys snapped to life independent of my faltering touch.

It was too late, about fifteen seconds too late. From the pool came a scream, a high and rising keening of bewildered agony, as of a child being hurt by witches in her dreams. Steve was holding her down in the chair, while Mike had spread her left hand on the tabletop and applied the jet from his blowtorch lighter to her nails. The red carnation polish had caught fire and was already burning rapidly with nasty, crackling little flames. I choked back the spurt of nausea in my throat and scrambled off the bench, with "Poet and Peasant" thundering along behind.

Max never knew. I hit him in the neck, where they'd taught me to hit them in basic-training camp, and he dropped like an ox with the butcher's mattock in its skull. I grabbed the gun before it bounced, and got Mike in the sights and yelled at him, the yell of a raving dipso in the alcoholic ward. He must have realized what was coming to him, no matter what, but he still had the lighter, and Lorna's right hand on the table spread out flat. He actually grinned at me and passed the flame across her nails once more and collapsed with my bullets tearing his grin to bloody shreds.

By that time the Big Fellow himself had a gun and was blasting away at me. He stood up to me all right, on his own two feet, still scowling angrily and firing from the hip. He couldn't be bothered running for cover from a stooge. But twenty yards is quite a distance to a man who has long been accustomed to having his killing done for him by the help. The Mauser's second burst sent him spinning into the diving board and ripped him apart.

Steve Kovacs confronted me with his arms flung high and a ghastly, fawning smile that told me he wanted to crawl right on over and lick my boots. Between us the girl crouched whimpering and sobbing on the tiles. She had quenched her flaming fingers in the pool, but her slender body still rocked and contorted itself from the pain. The cool night air scented with jasmine and sagebrush had been sharply tainted with a reek of gore and burned cordite.

From the desert came the fast-approaching roar of an engine bucking the cross-country grade, and almost instantly the jeep poked its blunt khaki nose through the tangerine brush. On the hood it displayed a crudely stenciled star, and the driver rising from behind the wheel was in faded brown denims and a khaki shirt. The moon caught a sparkle on his silver badge. He was hefting a shotgun, and pushing back his Stetson for a better look at us.

"Hold it! Police!"

His companion wore city clothes—gray slacks, tweed sports jacket. He came running on the balls of his feet, swerving briskly to circle the carnage on the tiles. His snub-nosed detective special wasn't picking any favorites yet, but I'd already clicked up the safety catch on the Mauser and was holding it out to him butt first. He snatched it away from me and gave me a puzzled stare.

"The musician!" he said, almost reverently surprised. "Now ain't that something for the book!"

It was only then that I dazedly recognized him: Sergeant Dettlinger, the cynical Formosa cop who'd dragged me from his nice clean gutter just the night before. Behind me the Blüthner struck its final crashing chord on the "Poet and Peasant" roll and relapsed into silence.

16

IT WAS EVE GARAND who practically ordered us to make a break for it.

She met us on the path below the tennis courts. She'd been running with the billowing skirts of her dinner gown clutched high above her knees, and her mannish gray hair flying out Valkyrie-like behind her neck. She insisted on shepherding us all the way to Lorna's bungalow while dragging the facts out of me in a rapid staccato of questions and sob-sister tricks.

"You'll have to get out," she told me crisply. "Both of you. Right now."

I frowned, and Lorna did not even hear. I was carrying her in my arms—she hadn't quite fainted, but she'd hardly have been capable of walking that far. They'd let us go, the sheriff's deputy and Dettlinger, to get her hands fixed up. They'd heard shots from the highway and come charging in, but now they were out of their depth, disorganized. The jeep was not equipped with radio: it had gone back to town for help. The Formosa detective had handcuffed Steve and Max together and waved us away as soon as he got the sketch. He'd come down with a warrant for Mike, who had been recognized that afternoon when he disposed of the Club Gaucho with a stink bomb and four sticks of dynamite.

"She needs a doctor," I reminded Eve. "And the cops took us off the leash because they figured we've no place to go. They don't even know about Stu Hitchcock yet."

"Young man, do you have money and a good fast car?"

We'd arrived at the cottage by then, and between us we were helping Lorna up the porch. It was the mentioning of money that jerked my thoughts back suddenly to Steve's black satchel, which still had to be in there with Vanni's one hundred and eighty grand they had intended to return to him. Because of his connections....

"Money," I said, somewhat bemusedly. "Yeah, we've got money. My car's an old wreck that'll do no more than sixty tops."

"You can use mine." She opened her bag and thrust keys into my hand. "It's in the yard, a Pontiac Grand Prix, last year's. Just leave it somewhere, mail these back to me. And that's not charity, my friend, just common decency. Start running and keep on the go—I presume you know where and how. If the rest of those mobsters catch up with you two they'll cut you up in little pieces."

She turned her back on me and carried Lorna off into the bedroom, soberly drawing her skirts aside to pass Stu's body where it blocked the arch. I checked my breath and looked around. The black satchel was there, on the little console where Steve had put it when he came in. Lips clenched between my teeth, I stared at it until it

seemed to fill the room. I had asked her to call
the man and make him bring some money for a
getaway, and here it was. Enough for both of us.
Enough to see us through the years of running,
through the years of danger, fear and constant
vigilance that lay ahead. His money or hers; it all
depended on your point of view or on whose
story you wanted to believe. If she had been his
niece. . . .

She'd denied having any family at all, but it occurred to me now that at the time she might not
have felt free to tell the truth. It was his secret
just as much as hers, and one she'd long been
taught to keep. He'd told me so himself, *all very
discreet, very confidential.* Yet he'd fooled me
deliberately, pretending he had no idea she was
here in Palm Springs. And she'd let me accuse
her with never a word of protest, as if it could
not possibly make any difference to us.

But that was just before the others had arrived.
I had crowded her, bullied her, proved to her
that the guy she loved was nothing but a bum
who had been hired to kick her heart around.
How could I expect a protest from her then?
There would have been no sense to it—a bum
does not care about the truth, and a murderess
can't afford it. I shrugged it off and concluded
the money was hers all right. She'd killed one
man with her own hands and another by biting
her tongue. It was only fair that she get something out of it, considering she'd have to take me
in the bargain.

She came out of the bedroom, wearing the
green silk suit and too much makeup, her finger-

tips neatly bandaged, trailing a racy scent of iodoform. She circled Stu's body and stepped across the poker without faltering, and stood before me lowering her eyes into the shadows. *All the things you are....*

"I'm ready, Rick," she told me quietly.

From the archway Eve Garand looked in on us, wiping her hands on a towel. "Be kind to her, Bailey," she prompted me, and her lean, clever features were gravely composed.

In the courtyard I found the Pontiac, and parked right next to it the low-slung, dusty gray Aston Martin that had clipped a fender off my car last Monday night. On the highway a distant red spotlight pricked the desert night. The sirens came shrilling in from town, five miles away.

17

HERE IN MY ROOM at the Cortez Hotel in El Paso I've switched on the desk lamp and rested my pen. It's getting dark outside, and I have spent all Sunday setting down these facts as clearly as my weary senses would allow. I had meant to conceal the result in the trunk of our new car, where the federal agents would have found it if the mob should find us first. But as it is I think I'll drop it in the mail to Eve, who'd be less hampered by formalities if it should come to counting up the chips.

I must wake Lorna now—when I looked in on her an hour ago she was still fast asleep. I've used the phone to order dinner for us, and a bottle of champagne. It means taking a chance on the room-service people connecting us, but we'll need that extra touch to brace ourselves against the strain. In an hour or so the weekend crowd will be hitting the roads, and we'll be pulling out of town with them. It is a thousand miles to New Orleans, and we must try to make it by tomorrow night. There are cargo tramps sailing for Kingston and Puerto Domingo and San Juan, and there's a man who owns a waterfront café, who used to be the bouncer at the Chien Qui Rit when I was playing there so many years ago.

18

SHE'S GONE....

I can't believe it, but she's gone. I went down the hall and scratched on the door of 1264, and walked on my toes into an empty room. She'd managed to dress herself somehow, and on the bed were my old yellow gloves and a note she'd painfully scribbled out on the back of a laundry list, because I'd used up all the paper in her desk. I stood looking at it in a daze, and then like a fool I rushed around searching the closet and the bath, scanning the street from the window, as if this were some crazy game of children's hide-and-seek. She's gone—she can't be far away, but it's hopeless trying to find her in this busy little city. She could be anywhere by now, in a drugstore, taxi, rooming house, movie, anywhere at all. She may be on a train, or in jail with those bandages of hers worn openly. Or in the morgue, if *they* have spotted her. I should never have left her alone, not for a minute, regardless of the risk.

The note doesn't help. I've taken it back to 1259, and I've been staring at it ever since, until the words are nothing but a blur.

Rick, it's no use. You cannot love me as I am, for what you think I am. You only feel you must make up for what you were compelled to do to me. How can I go with you, knowing that now you'd marry me just so they could not make you testify to what you saw? You said last night you would "pick up the check" for me, but I won't let you, darling, I just won't, that's all.

She means to go back, of course, see it through by herself. She has some money in her purse, perhaps enough to take a plane. If she tried that, they've already arrested her. In that case they'd be here now—no, they wouldn't; she'd refuse to tell them where I am. At the railroad station or the bus depot she might slip by. They won't be watching westbound traffic very closely. Her best bet would be hitching a ride, almost the only way she could expect to travel back to California without a matron pushing her around. Maybe I should get out the car and start driving west on the chance of heading her off— Oh, God, it's dark and there must be at least three different roads she could be on. She doesn't realize what she'll be up against. I've got to stop her in some way, I've got to do something. *I've got to do something.*

19

I'VE JUST PHONED MARION. It does sound like a
crazy thing to do, but I remembered that her boss
knows the big politicians and calls the governor
by his first name.

The circuit was humming and buzzing, twelve
hundred miles across the vast, eroded plains, the
cactus-covered mesa and the snow-topped mountains, through the cattle towns, the oil towns,
the railroad towns—Las Cruces, Lordsburg, Tuc-
son, El Centro, Pomona—to a click and a strange,
gruff masculine voice saying hello, noncommit-
tally blunt, and the operator's sweetly officious
western drawl demanding Miss Marion Faraday,
please.

"Who wants her?"

"El Paso callin'." The dulcet vowels had grown
tart. "Is Miss Faraday theah, please, suh?"

I almost hung up in despair, but it wouldn't
have done any good; the fat was in the fire. I
heard a mutter at the other end, and then
Marion's voice sounding tense and excited. "Yes,
who is it?"

"Ready with Los Angeles," the operator told
me coldly, clicking out.

For a moment the line hummed emptily while

the sweat coursed down my spine and the knuckles cracked in my hand where it gripped the receiver. "Sure you want to know?" I asked her finally, when I managed to choke up the words.

"Rick, where are you? Are you all right? Oh, my dearest, my love, what's happened to you, why did you go away? That awful woman.... Are you alone?"

"Yeah, I'm alone."

"Oh, I'm so glad you called! You've packed her off, haven't you, Rick? You're coming back, aren't you?"

"Take it easy," I said. "Who was that answering your phone?"

"My bodyguard. Now aren't you proud of me? There's a man and a woman from the governor's crime commission here all the time. Mr. Jeffries arranged for it, right after the coroner's jury adjourned last night. Oh, darling, you've got to be careful for the next few days, until they round up all those filthy gangsters. You'd better go straight to the F.B.I. and let them put you on a plane, and we'll protect you here when you arrive."

"Protect me, hell," I said. "You'll protect me right into the clink and throw the key away, that's how you'll protect me."

"But, Rick, they've excused you. The jury says it was all done in self-defense!" She was crying now, and laughing, and shouting at me. "Darling, where have you been? It's on the radio, in the newspapers, everywhere! Don't you realize what a terrific break this is for you, this grand publicity and everything? You'll be able to start your band again and get hundreds of offers for jobs, and people will fall over themselves to listen to you play. I heard the coroner myself when he called you a hero!''

I tugged at my collar and tore at my hair in dismay. The local Sunday paper lay beside me on the floor. I'd bought it off the stand at 6:00 A.M.; it was probably an early edition, printed on Saturday afternoon. "That's just dandy!'' I yelled back at her. "What were you doing there? How did you ever get mixed up in this?''

"You don't need to worry, Rick, the jury cleared me, too,'' she assured me earnestly. "They said it was only an accident, when he cursed me and hit me and threatened to kill me, and I grabbed the poker and hit him back with it. I was looking for you, because Pablo had noticed a sticker from this hotel in Palm Springs on the windshield of your car. So on Friday I left the office early and drove out, and a bellboy pointed out your bungalow to me. But he made a mistake, and I walked into that awful woman's apartment, and I found Stu Hitchcock there, and he said you were out with her. He was nasty about it at first, but then he suddenly got ideas, about both of us being alone in there, getting the runaround together. That's when he made a pass at me, of all the stupid things to do, and I finally had to hint at something you'd told me, about him being just a silly college boy you'd been hired to get out of a mess, and that's how we got into this horrible fight. So of course I was terribly scared at first and I drove all the way back home,

but in the morning I saw Mr. Jeffries and we both
decided I should go to Riverside and give myself
up at the inquest. Rick, what's the matter? Can
you hear me, darling? Are you still there?''

I hung up and sat on the bed for a while, trying
to dig my fingers deep into my head. The phone
started ringing again almost immediately and
kept it up at intervals for another ten minutes or
so. I went back to the desk at last, and I've spent
some little time on writing all this down, for no
good reason anymore. I suppose Dr. Hirsch would
approve; he always made us do it at the hospital,
whatever bothered us, down to the last detail.
Then he'd kid us along about how he was going
to sell it to the movies and charge us ten-percent
commission on the deal.

He could not sell this one; they tell me irony is
poison to the customers. And the worst of it is
where she must have believed that Vanni killed
the boy. That's why she bit her tongue, to all of
us. There was nothing to say; in her philosophy
the truth's disloyalty would have defeated her as
badly as the self-conviction of a lie. *Rick, it's no
use....*

There's a knock on the door. Room service has
been slow. I guess they needed time to cool the
wine.

20

SX 115 (ATTN. L.A., HW, PS)

URGENT

1ST LEAD BAILEY SHOOTING

BY KENNETH FOSTER, UNITED PRESS INTERNATIONAL STAFF CORRESPONDENT EL PASO, TEX, MARCH 27 - (UPI) - RICHARD L. BAILEY, HEROIC SLAYER OF CALIFORNIA GAMBLING BOSS WALTER HITCHCOCK, WAS HOSPITALIZED AT 7:45 P.M. TODAY IN CRITICAL CONDITION AT EL PASO SISTERS OF MERCY FOLLOWING A SECOND SHOOTING AFFRAY IN A LOCAL HOTEL. POLICE AND FBI, WHO HAD BEEN TIPPED TO THE IMPENDING TRAGEDY, ARRIVED IN TIME TO ARREST NICK MAROS, 44, OF PHOENIX, ARIZONA, AS HE ATTEMPTED TO MAKE HIS ESCAPE INTO THE STREET, AND JAIL HIM ON SUSPICION OF ASSAULT WITH INTENT TO KILL. IN BAILEY'S ROOM THEY FOUND THE FORMER VETERAN, NOW A HOLLYWOOD SALESMAN, UNCONSCIOUS WITH A FRACTURED SKULL AND BULLET WOUNDS IN THE ABDOMEN AND IN BOTH LEGS. BESIDE HIM LAY THE LIFELESS BODY OF STEPHEN S. KOVACS, 51, OF BEL AIR, CALIFORNIA, HITCHCOCK HENCHMAN, WHO ESCAPED FROM THE RIVERSIDE COUNTY JAIL DURING SATURDAY NIGHT WHILE BEING HELD FOR INVESTIGATION IN THE PALM SPRINGS POOLSIDE DEATH OF MOTION PICTURE STAR ALFREDO VANNI. EL PASO POLICE CHIEF PAT MCCALL SAID BAILEY APPEARED TO HAVE ADMITTED BOTH MEN, DESCRIBED AS GANGLAND HIT MEN, TO HIS ROOM, AND A STRUGGLE DEVELOPED, IN THE

COURSE OF WHICH, THOUGH ALREADY SEVERELY WOUNDED
HIMSELF, HE SUCCEEDED IN WRESTLING AWAY KOVACS'S
GUN, A .45 COLT AUTOMATIC, AND SHOOTING ITS OWNER
THROUGH THE HEART.

LP815P

SX116

SAN FRANCISCO, MARCH 29 - (UPI) - SATURDAY LIVESTOCK
REPEAT:

CATTLE SALABLE 1,200. SUPPLY INCLUDED AROUND 11
LOAD STEERS. TRADE OPENED VERY SLOW WITH PRICES
GENERALLY STEADY ON FEW SCATTERED SALES. LOAD HIGH-
MEDIUM 890-LB STEERS 24, SOME MEDIUM 1025-1070-LB
STEERS 22-22.50. MEDIUM HEIFERS 17-21. CALVES 275. NO
EARLY SALES.

HT827P

SX117 (LP TO PX)

CORRECTION

IN BAILEY SHOOTING EL PASO READ IT NICK MARCOS
(STED MAROS)

LP831P

HW 26S TO LP

PRESSURING FULLEST ON BAILEY PLS URGENT

HW832P

SX 118

YR 1147A SAT: BUREAU RECLAMATION SEZ NO SALTWATER
BARRIER SURVEY BEING MADE DUE LACK PERSONNEL BUT
ONE AUTHORIZED UNDER WELCH RESOLUTION 86TH
CONGRESS, WHICH ORDERED COMPLETE STUDY BAY AREA
WATER PROBLEMS.
BC 19 M839P

HW 27A TO LP

SIGNALS OVER WILL YOU GUYS HURRY UP PLS LA CONCUR

HW 842P

SX 119

HW, LA

ADD BAILEY SHOOTING EL PASO XXX HEART.

HOTEL WORKERS ASSERT BAILEY REGISTERED SATURDAY
ABOUT 1:00 P.M. AS DONALD WELLS OF NYC RENTING SUITE ON
TWELFTH FLOOR, SOON AFTER WOMAN HAD REGISTERED ON
SAME FLOOR AS MRS. MARY HENDRICKS OF BTM. CHIEF
MCCALL TENTATIVELY IDENTIFIED THIS WOMAN AS LORNA
RYAN, MOTION PICTURE ACTRESS AND THE SECOND MISSING
WITNESS IN FRIDAY'S PALM SPRINGS TRAGEDY. MRS.
HENDRICKS HAD LEFT THE HOTEL BEFORE THE AFFRAY.

LP 849P

HW 28S TO LP

TIPPED CONFIDENTIALLY RYAN GIRL NOT ACTRESS BUT
VANNI'S ILLEGITIMATE DAUGHTER. CHECK WHEN PSBL PLS.
MORE

HW 854P

SX 120

ADD BAILEY SHOOTING EL PASO XXX AFFRAY.

FBI AGENT IN CHARGE JOHN HARRIS REFUSED COMMENT ON
REPORTS THAT A LARGE SUM OF MONEY HAD BEEN FOUND IN
BAILEY'S LUGGAGE. INQUIRIES AT SISTERS OF MERCY
HOSPITAL ELICITED HIS INJURIES ARE OF A GRAVE NATURE
AND HE MAY NOT REGAIN CONSCIOUSNESS, THOUGH
EMERGENCY OPERATIONS FOR REMOVAL OF THREE .45
CALIBER BULLETS HAVE BEEN SUCCESSFULLY
ACCOMPLISHED. XXX HOLD FOR FLASH XXX. FLASH: LORNA
RYAN, 20, MISSING WITNESS IN FRIDAY'S PALM SPRINGS

POOLSIDE TRAGEDY, WAS LOCATED HERE WHEN SHE
RETURNED TO THE HOTEL WHERE SHE HAD BEEN REGISTERED
WITH BAILEY UNDER ANOTHER NAME. MISS RYAN EXPRESSED
INSTANT CONCERN WHEN INFORMED OF THE INCIDENT AND
STATED TEARFULLY THAT BAILEY IS HER FIANCE. SHE WAS
RUSHED TO THE HOSPITAL IN A POLICE CAR BY CITY
DETECTIVES H.J. WILLAMETTE AND WILLIAM LYNCH.

LP 902P

HW 29S TO LP
   CHECK OUR 28S WHEN PSBL PLS. IMPORTANT. MORE.

HW 903P

21

THE RAGGED YELLOW COIL of teletype carbon
spilled across my blankets and almost into Lorna's
lap where she'd sat beside me for the best part of
the past three days. The UPI man watched us quiz-
zically, straddling a chair at the foot of the bed
and ducking the weights on pulleys that were
keeping the splint on my leg under traction where
one slug had cracked a tibia. He was a tall, broad-
shouldered, straw-blond young Texan who
looked slightly uncomfortable in his neatly
pressed city clothes. His drawl brought up images
of oil derricks, and pearl-handled six guns.

"Ah reckon that last one theah might be the
sixty-fo'-dollah question for me to ask y'all," he
observed cheerfully. "Ah've been pahkin' on
yore doorstep, waitin' all this while till the
sawbones'd let me in. Cain't help mahself—they
want the answer awful bad, out California ways."

"No comment," I said.

He winced a little. Lorna frowned at me and
gently touched the helmet dressing's stiff white
folds where they encased my head above the ears.

"Off the record," I said, "I don't know. I don't
want to know. Miss Ryan offered to tell me and I
shut her up. That may not make sense to you, but

it happens to be the way I feel about it. This confidential tip your Hollywood office claims to have may be the McCoy or it may be just another publicity deal, I don't care which. You'll never be able to print it, not without her confirmation and consent. If there had to be a trial, and she were forced to disclose her relationship to Mr. Vanni on the witness stand, that might be a different matter, but as it is there's nobody left to try. Not where she's concerned."

He actually had the effrontery to wink at me. "You did a job of makin' shore of that."

"Wanna make something out of it?"

The bandaged fingertips brushed my lips and the cool, childish little voice said anxiously, "Darling, please. . . ." I relaxed and felt less like a consummate idiot.

The UPI man said, "No offense, suh, no offense. Ah kin see how y'all might look at this heah situation. Reckon you sho 'nuff earned the right to have a little privacy, the hahd way. How'd this fellow from Phoenix know wheah to catch up with y'all, kin you tell me?"

"You'd better ask Harris or chief McCall," I said. "They may not want to turn up cards just yet. That part of it will show in court all right."

I knew, of course—it had been an easy guess, the very instant I recognized the long-nosed drunk pushing into my room at the Cortez with Kovacs on his heels. The F.B.I. had squeezed the story out of him, and Harris had been frank with me about it, even if his own face had been red and he'd hated to knock the Riverside County cops. They'd taken Kovacs out through the Hacienda parking lot that Friday night, and there he'd noticed that Stu's car was gone. He was the only one to spot it right away; not even Sergeant Dettlinger caught on, and Max Gonzalez had been on a stretcher with a broken neck. So when they booked him, and they let him use the courthouse phone, according to the rules, he spilled a mouthful of Hungarian on the wires before they cut him short, and long before I'd covered those three hundred miles and ditched the Aston Martin in the basement of the Westward Ho. By that time there must have been three dozen hoods like Marcos laying for us, all the way from San Francisco through Las Vegas to the Rio Grande. Harris had told me that in California alone, federal agents and the crime commission had made sixty-five arrests.

The UPI man grinned at me knowingly and inquired, "How long are these heah sawbones aimin' to keep you laid up, Mistuh Bailey?"

"They won't commit themselves. I'm supposed to be lucky they sent back the hearse."

"Makin' any plans for when they let you go?"

"Back to pounding the pavements, I guess, and selling more greeting cards," I said, returning his grin with interest.

He chuckled self-consciously and protested, "Uh-uh. Ah've since had time to do a little checkin' on you, suh."

The tall, spare colonel from Special Services cleared his throat. He'd been resting against the mantelpiece and watching us in sober amusement. "You can quote me that Sergeant Bailey's going back into the Army," he said sharply.

"We'll get up a band of servicemen for him and
send him on a tour of hospitals and foreign bases
for a year or two. After that it'll be up to him."

I could feel Lorna's hand draw tight in mine
and smiled at her, probably rather foolishly. The
UPI man just nodded and glanced at his notes. I
was quite sure he meant to ask about the money
next, but instead he came up with a real corker.
"If you'll pahdon me, ma'am, Ah'm supposed to
find out wheah you'd gone when these fellows
came in afeudin' after y'all."

"Don't answer that!" I snapped, but she sat up
very straight and faced him as serenely as if he'd
paid her something of a compliment.

"I was frightened," she told him in a calm,
clear voice. "I didn't think I could stand it, the
running and hiding we'd have to do. Then I took
a walk and changed my mind."

He stared at her dubiously as if he did not trust
his ears. There was a quick, fussy tap-tap-tap on
the door, and one of the sisters fluttered in,
clutching nervously at the rustling skirts of her
starched white habit. The kindly wrinkled oval
of her face was rosy with excitement.

"Please, sir, Father Dominic is here, and the TV
people, and the other reporters, and all those
photographers want to take pictures. . . ."

The UPI man was groping through his pockets
in sudden comical distress. He found what he
was looking for and held it up for us to see.

"Ah got the boys to chip in with me," he
declared embarrassedly. "We reckoned y'all'd be
shore to fo'get about the ring."

Be a detective.
See if you can solve...

Raven House
MINUTE
MYSTERY #3

On the following page is Raven House
MINUTE MYSTERY #3, "Alibi."

Every month each Raven House book will feature a
MINUTE MYSTERY, a unique little puzzler designed
to let *you* do the sleuthing!

U.S. (except Arizona) residents may check their
answer by calling **1-800-528-1404** during the
months of January and February 1982. U.S.
residents may also obtain the solution by writing
anytime during or after this period to:

   Raven House MINUTE MYSTERY
   1440 South Priest Drive
   Tempe, AZ 85281

Canadian residents, please write to the following
address:

   Raven House MINUTE MYSTERY
   649 Ontario Street
   Stratford, Ontario N5A 6W2

ALIBI

The professor was in an expansive mood.

"I've often observed," he told his dinner guests, "how extremely difficult it is to fake an unassisted alibi. The recent Werner affair in Chicago is a case in point."

He fired a cigar and continued. "I had no suspicion of Werner when I bumped into him on Michigan Avenue the morning after a friend of his had been found murdered. When I casually inquired where he'd been between four and six o'clock the previous afternoon, he gave the following account.

"'It was such a glorious afternoon that about two o'clock I went for a sail. When I was about eight miles offshore—about 5:30—the wind died down completely. There wasn't a breath of air. Drifting about I recalled that the international distress signal is a flag flown upside down, so I ran mine to the top of the mast in that manner and waited in the dead calm.

"'Shortly after six o'clock the freighter, *Luella*, heaved to, and I went aboard her after securing my boat with a towline. Her skipper said he'd seen my distress signal about three miles away. He put me ashore at Harvey's Landing, and a passing car gave me a lift to town. Imagine my surprise when I read in the morning paper that the *Luella* had sunk in a storm last night and all hands had been lost!'"

The professor sipped his wine and went on. "While the *Luella* had been sunk with loss of entire crew, I immediately arrested Werner for further questioning. I knew his alibi was faked."

How did the professor know?

From **Minute Mysteries** by Austin Ripley.
Copyright © 1949 by Opera Mundi, Paris.